Prologue

1810

Rose peered down from the highest branches of the oak tree. 'See, Millie, they *are* coming this way.'

Her twin shifted nervously on her perch. 'I said we shouldn't climb this tree, Papa will be furious. Whilst Mama is away we are supposed to be on our best behaviour, not scrambling about in the tops of trees like village children.'

Rose giggled and let the branches drop. When their brother, David, had arrived for an unexpected visit bringing two friends with him, she had been determined to view them for herself. There was little likelihood she, or her sister, would get an opportunity to meet them. Such lofty members of society as these two young gentlemen would not wish to be introduced to a pair of

1

schoolgirls; she and Millie were well below their notice.

When David was home he always strolled around the park after breakfast. From the vantage point of the ancient oak they would be able to stare without being observed. At least that had been the plan, but if Millie continued her wriggling they would shortly be discovered. Although this escapade, as always, had been at her instigation, this time she did not wish to be found culpable.

David would laugh and the fair gentleman with merry blue eyes would also take it in good part. The tallest of the three, the one with raven black hair and scowling features, concerned her. She did not wish to be in his black books. Before Rose could stop her, Millie scrambled to a lower branch and sat, her legs dangling, waiting to be seen. Rose pressed herself into the shadows and prayed she would remain undetected.

'What have we here?' It wasn't David who had stopped but the fair gentleman. 'A damsel in distress. Come, fair

MISS BANNERMAN
AND THE DUKE

A marriage of convenience to Peregrine, the Marquis of Bentley, is the only way Rose Bannerman can save her family from ruin — her twin, Millie, is too sensitive for such an undertaking. However, Rose finds Perry arrogant and proud, while he thinks Rose pert and impolite. He considers Millie a more suitable bride but when Rose takes her sister's place, her actions compromise them both. Lord Bentley is obliged to offer an arrangement neither party is happy with . . .

FENELLA MILLER

MISS BANNERMAN AND THE DUKE

Complete and Unabridged

LINFORD
Leicester

First published in Great Britain in 2012

First Linford Edition
published 2012

British Library CIP Data

Miller, Fenella-Jane.
 Miss Bannerman and the duke. - -
(Linford romance library)
1. Love stories.
2. Large type books.
I. Title II. Series
823.9′2–dc23

ISBN 978–1–4448–1182–7

Published by
F. A. Thorpe (Publishing)
Anstey, Leicestershire

Set by Words & Graphics Ltd.
Anstey, Leicestershire
Printed and bound in Great Britain by
T. J. International Ltd., Padstow, Cornwall

This book is printed on acid-free paper

maiden, allow me to rescue you.'

Millie dropped like a stone into his arms. It would have seemed to those below she had done it deliberately. Rose knew her sister had lost her grip and fallen from her perch inadvertently. The young man staggered but somehow remained on his feet — after all Millie was not a huge weight.

'I beg your pardon, sir; I slipped.' Millie's glorious blonde curls had escaped from their restraining ribbon and were tumbling about her shoulders. Everyone said how different the sisters were, not identical in any way. At thirteen years of age Millie was already a beauty; she looked like their mama whilst Rose was the image of their father.

'Millie, you're incorrigible. Miss Evans will be most displeased. You had best run along to the schoolroom directly,' David said sternly.

Suitably chastened, Millie dropped her head, curtsied and then hurried away without a second thought. The bark was cutting into Rose's palms. *Why didn't they move on?* She wished she'd not climbed quite so high, wished she'd not been left to scramble down alone.

Her brother informed his friends, 'That was Amelia. I expect Rosamond had more sense than to climb a tree.'

The fair gentleman replied as he brushed himself free of debris, 'She will turn a few heads when she's out. To have such beauty, be of impeccable breeding and with a substantial dowry — you will have your work cut out keeping her safe, David.'

Rose pressed her cheek against the trunk waiting until she could safely descend. The voices faded. They must be far enough away for her to attempt to get down. She tried to let go, to swing around and lower her slippers to the next branch. Her limbs refused to obey her commands. She was frozen to the spot. A slight noise below made her cling on all the tighter. She clenched her teeth to hold back a whimper of fear.

'Sit still, child, I shall have you down

safely in a moment.' A lean brown hand reached up and prised her rigid fingers from their grip. 'Relax, little one, I shall not drop you. Allow me to turn you round, then put your arms around my neck and your legs around my waist and I shall have you on the ground in no time at all.'

His hands were warm, strong and capable. Rose's fear trickled away and she let him do as he had suggested. With her face resting against his collar she inhaled a comforting mix of lemon soap and horses. She kept her eyes firmly closed and hung on for grim death until her world stopped moving.

'There, as promised, back on terra firma. You can open your eyes and let go, you are safe.' Her fingers unclenched and she was lowered gently to the path, but the firm hold on her upper arms remained. 'Look at me. I wish to see the face of the young lady I risked my life and limbs to rescue.'

Reluctantly Rose raised her head. She already knew who she would see; it could only be the saturnine gentleman for her brother and the fair one had long gone.

'Thank you, sir, I'm not usually so chickenhearted. I cannot think why I couldn't scramble down this time.'

He smiled. He looked quite different when he did so, almost handsome in a devilish kind of way. 'That was a prodigious height you climbed. Perhaps you will not be so easily persuaded next time?'

Good grief! He thought the escapade Millie's idea. She would not disabuse him; he might become the formidable stranger she had spied from her perch. Dropping into a graceful curtsey she mumbled a second thank you and sped away before he could question her further.

* * *

Perry watched the girl he'd just carried down from the tree through narrowed eyes. She was as unlike her twin as chalk was to cheese. Where Amelia had periwinkle blue eyes, golden curls and already showed signs of a pleasing form, Rosamond had plain mouse-brown hair and was thin as a stick. But there was something about the girl that intrigued him. He had seen intelligence in her remarkable violet eyes. His lips twitched. If he was honest he would, like most gentlemen, select the more lively sister, the one who had instigated the tree climbing and not her quieter, plainer sibling.

'Perry, where the devil are you?'

'David, I'm coming. Did you know that this is a Turkey oak? You can detect this species by examining the foliage.'

His host clapped him on the shoulder. 'I might have known something like that would catch your interest. Already you're becoming a dry old stick, and you only three and twenty.'

1

1815

'Mama, why do I have to attend this ball? Why not put an advertisement in The Times instead?'

'Rose, my love, I do wish you would not say such things. You know I'm depending on you or Millie to make an advantageous marriage. If you do not your brother shall inherit a bankrupt title and estate.'

'Exactly so — as it is the wealth of my future husband that is paramount, why do I have to go through the bother of parading like a prize mare at Tattersall's? If they present their credentials, you can select one for me.'

Her sister dabbed her eyes with a miniscule cotton square. 'How can you make fun of our situation, Rose? I cannot bear the thought of marrying without affection. I'm praying that I shall be able to love my future husband, whatever the reasons behind our nuptials.'

Rose smiled. 'Then it's up to me to be less choosy. For you, dearest, it is quite different. You are bound to be the most beautiful young woman at Almack's tonight, and you will have a dozen suitors banging on the door tomorrow morning. Surely you can fall in love with one of them?'

'If you would only smile and pretend to be enjoying yourself you might also attract someone pleasant.'

Rose noticed her sister did not suggest it would be anyone eligible, or even attractive. No, her lot was to marry an elderly widower with a brood of children needing a step-mama. Ah well! As long as he had very deep pockets and left her to her own devices, she would be content.

'A gentleman does not like to be stared at so disdainfully even from someone as lovely as you,' her sister chided.

'When at your side, Millie, I become

invisible. I will own that I have handsome eyes, a trim figure and an abundance of shiny brown hair but my appearance is not fashionable. Being a diminutive golden goddess is essential for success in the *ton* this season.' She stared thoughtfully at her reflection in the mantel mirror. 'I am several inches taller than you. That, combined with my lack of fair hair, is more than enough to deter all but the most desperate of suitors.'

She shrugged and turned away; appearances were not everything, she knew. There was only one man who stirred her heart, and he could not be called a truly handsome man by all but the most besotted of mamas. And unfortunately, neither was he to be found where she was bound that night.

Rose had never forgotten the gentleman who had climbed up the oak tree to rescue her all those years ago. Peregrine Adolphus Edward Sinclair, Marquis of Bentley, Duke of Essex — his name as impressive as himself.

He was too top lofty to consider either of them as his bride. She doubted he would attend the marriage mart. From what she had learned about the Duke he was easily bored and only attended the occasional ball or soiree.

Her maid shook out an invisible crease in her gown. 'There, Miss Rose, you look a picture. Lavender silk complements your eyes.' The girl handed over the matching reticule and fan and then stood back to admire her handiwork.

Millie, beautiful in the palest gold sarcenet, smiled sympathetically. 'I know; too many flounces and rouleau. The gown would have suited you better if the modiste had made it plain, the way you requested it.'

'I look ridiculous. I know it, and so shall every other person at Almack's tonight. If Papa was not still abroad on business, he would have taken my part.' She frowned. 'In fact, this scheme of our mother's does not have his blessing. I hope he appreciates the sacrifice I'm going to make.'

On cue, their mama rustled in, magnificent in purple silk, the egret feathers on her turban bobbing wildly.

'Come, girls, we must not keep the horses standing. Do try and look happy, Rosamond. I declare you will scare away the gentlemen frowning like that.'

'Let us hope so,' said Rose, raising an elegant eyebrow at her sister.

The only fortunate aspect of their reduced circumstances was the fact that they had not had their own come-out ball. They had attended a few select musical evenings and soirees, but this was to be their first fully public event. The best Rose could hope for was to be ignored; the worst was to be asked to dance and reveal that not only was she dressed like a maypole, she danced like one too.

Her mother was an inveterate card player — fortunately not a gambler — so would join other like-minded matrons in an ante-room as soon as she and Millie had been introduced to a few gentlemen. Rose intended to slip away and hide behind a curtain where she could read the new novel she had secreted in her reticule. Her sister was a sensible girl and would behave with the utmost rectitude. Rose was more likely to do something to scandalise society.

If only David had not accompanied their papa; he was well established in Town and could have introduced Millie to several of his friends. Her heart skipped a beat. There was only one of his friends she wanted to be formally introduced to and there was no chance of that. Her feelings for this man could be no more than an infatuation; after all, she had only met him that once and he would surely have forgotten all about her.

Without any prompting her brother had, on his frequent visits, kept them up to date with the exploits of his friends. The fair gentleman was the Hon. Richard Devonshire, oldest son of Lord Devonshire, no more than comfortably situated. *Her* gentleman, despite his not being in the accepted mode, could pick and choose his bride. No young lady would quibble if a Duke offered for her. The fact that he was a young and vigorous man, rather than an elderly roué, would only add to his eligibility. He was, most certainly, the catch of the season.

Knowing full well the impossibility of marrying the man who had occupied her thoughts for the past five years, Rose decided she would forfeit herself on the altar of matrimony for the good of her family. Darling Millie was far too susceptible, too sensitive to be asked to marry someone she did not love. The fact that marriage would involve unpleasant intimacies was something Rose pushed firmly to the back of her mind.

★   ★   ★

'Perry, I implore you, think about this. You will be nine and twenty next month and are the last of your line. It would be catastrophic if you died without an heir. That doesn't bear thinking about; if there is a next in line somewhere he is so far removed from us he will be impossible.'

'Laura, my dear, I'm not about to kick the bucket. I'm in my prime, I've plenty of time to set up my nursery.' Perry eyed his older sister with disfavour. He was heartily sick of being berated for his lack of interest in finding a wife. 'However, as today *is* your name day, I shall agree, just this once, to attend Almack's tonight — even though the food is inedible, the wine undrinkable and the company not much better. Really, I would rather have my teeth pulled.'

Obviously satisfied now she had achieved her aim, Laura chose to ignore his last remark. 'If you will stand up with Emma she is guaranteed a successful season. What point is there of having a Duke for an uncle if he is not there to sponsor his niece?'

This was too much. 'Heavens above, Laura, am I not paying for her season? Have I not opened up my townhouse for you? Am I not to hold a ball in her honour in a few weeks time?'

He frowned, no longer amused by this conversation. 'I have business to attend to; I shall not accompany you to that wretched place, but you have my word I shall put in an appearance at some point.'

'I beg your pardon. I did not wish to offend you.'

He stared down his nose at her and added, 'I do not, however, intend to dance. Just being there is punishment enough.'

Perry strode off. The thought of having to wear knee breeches and silk stockings appalled him. He had adopted the recent fashion of pantaloons and evening shoes — far more comfortable — and he resented being obliged to change his style in order to be let into that place. He had heard rumours at his club that Wellington himself had been refused entry for turning up incorrectly dressed.

That's what came from allowing women too much power. The three ladies who ruled the roost at Almack's were not to his taste. When he did eventually become leg-shackled he would make very sure his bride was biddable. He grinned. The notion was an impossible conundrum. He doubted there was a young lady in London who would meet his stringent requirements. First, to be obedient to his wishes and second, to have a lively personality and ready wit. In his experience — and in these past six years it had been extensive — he had discovered one either got obedience or wit — never both. He chuckled as he recalled a young lady he'd been introduced to three years ago. If she hadn't been reminiscent of a bovine she would have suited him perfectly. He must add a third requirement to his list: the young lady he would choose must also be reasonably attractive.

★　★　★

Rose had curtsied and smiled until her face ached. She had considered adopting a limp, thus preventing any partners from asking her to dance, but that would be unfair to Mama and Millie. The two were already sorely afflicted by being accompanied by an over-decorated beanpole; for the beanpole also to be infirm would be the outside of enough. So she adopted the expression of a frightened rabbit, starting at every comment and looking away and fussing with her reticule and fan as if too shy to contemplate an answer. This combination had put off even the bravest of souls.

'Rosamond, I'm in despair at your behaviour tonight. Thank the Lord your sister is more accommodating. See how she's enjoying herself? Would you not like to be dancing as she is?'

'No, Mama, I would not. I am sufficiently conspicuous lurking here in the shadows. Imagine my chagrin if I were to be exposed in this hideous garment in the centre of the dance floor?'

Her mama threw up her hands in despair. 'You would not behave this way if your papa was here.'

'I would not be here at all if he was home. Why don't you join your friends for a game of whist? I shall be perfectly safe behind this pillar. Millie will come to no harm now she is under the protection of Lady Eleanor Dashwood. It is fortuitous an old school friend of yours is here to act as chaperone.'

Thus assured, her mother vanished in the crowd and Rose was about to creep away to find herself a private corner when she overheard a group of young gentlemen.

'Hard to credit that they come from the same family, let alone are twins. Miss Amelia Bannerman is the loveliest creature, yet her sister is an antidote.'

'I think she's touched in the attic. Imagine looking like she does and also being a simpleton.'

Rose stiffened. There could be no doubt at all to whom they were referring. How dare they discuss her in this way? She stiffened, her eyes flashing. They would not get away with this insult.

2

Caught up in her anger at the overheard comments, Rose was startled when a dark-featured gentleman appeared at her side. 'Miss Rose, would you do me the honour of joining me in the next set?'

Who was he? Suddenly she recognised him and her hands clenched. The Duke's abrupt appearance flustered her and she was unable to do more than shake her head, the power of speech temporarily deserting her. He smiled.

'I heard what those idiots were saying. How better to prove them wrong than by dancing with me?'

Her voice returned. 'I cannot see how that will improve the situation.'

'I never dance, my dear. For me to honour you in this way will guarantee you a successful season.'

'One dance will make me a success?'

'Naturally. If I think you a suitable

partner then so will the rest of the *ton*.'

'I thank you, your Grace, but I have no wish to be considered suitable. Pray excuse me . . . '

His eyes narrowed and the grip on the arm tightened. 'You forget yourself, Miss Bannerman. I've invited you to dance and you will not refuse me.'

Scarcely able to believe her ears, Rose stared at him. He was surely jesting? His expression made it plain he was not. How could she have thought this man so special when he was little more than an arrogant aristocrat? He had no right to dragoon her into something she did not wish to do, just because he believed himself to be important. She tried to hang back but he continued to march her ahead towards the dance floor. *What could she do?* People were already smiling behind her back, and she could not create a scene by openly struggling.

Other couples were milling about on the floor forming squares to begin the next dance and his hold relaxed. He must believe she'd submitted to his demands. Before he could stop her she removed her arm from his. 'Thank you, your Grace, but I do not dance either. Please excuse me; I am certain you will find another young lady eager to accompany such an illustrious gentleman as yourself.'

No well brought up young lady abandoned their partner so rudely. She was facing social ruin, but she didn't care. Her childish dreams were shattered; the man she had thought the epitome of gallantry was no different from any other man. He was shallow and conceited, stuffed full of his own importance, determined to have his way regardless of her feelings. One dance with him would not miraculously turn her from an ugly duckling into a swan.

Leaving him adrift on the edge of the ballroom, his humiliation noted by everyone, she quickly threaded her way through the throng and into the hall. There must be somewhere she could hide until the ball was over?

Perry felt the eyes of several tabbies boring into him. Forcing down his fury, he shrugged and smiled vaguely in their direction. 'How unfortunate! Miss Bannerman *did* say she could not dance just yet — I had not realized how urgent the matter was. I shall wait for her to return and *then* we shall dance.'

He strolled away, nodding and smiling as appropriate, but his eyes were scanning the crowds searching for the missing girl.

How dare she make him look a fool?

He had not wished to dance with her, had stepped in to save her from total humiliation. She repaid his gallant gesture by abandoning him. When he found her she would regret her foolhardy action. He shouldered his way through the press on the edge of the ballroom. Acquaintances hailed him. He ignored them.

Where was the dratted girl?

Downstairs there were retiring rooms,

she might well be there. An unfortunate footman blocked his passage. He glared and the young man stepped aside so smartly his wig tipped over one eye. Perry strode on determined to find his quarry.

★ ★ ★

The hall was all but deserted. After ten o'clock no one was admitted through these hallowed doors.

Where could she hide?

There were columns aplenty but none big enough for her to remain out of sight and read her book in peace. Perhaps she could claim she had a headache and spend the remainder of the evening in the ladies' retiring chamber? These rooms should be easy enough to find as there would be a constant stream of young ladies in and out.

Sure enough, she spied her destination on the ground floor. She slipped through the hall and ran downstairs. She was in sight of her objective when, to her horror, the Duke materialised in front of her. He did not look at all pleased to see her; in fact he looked furious. She stopped so suddenly her toes were crushed in her dance slippers. Not daring to meet his fulminating stare she dropped her eyes and clutched her reticule protectively to her chest.

What could she say to avert this disaster?

Her breathing steadied as a simple solution occurred to her. She dipped in a deep curtsey. 'Are you very angry with me, sir? I tried to tell you: I do not like to dance and especially not in this ensemble. I am already a laughing stock, and stumbling around the dance floor would only add to my unhappiness. I do most humbly beg your pardon if I have caused you any embarrassment.'

A well-remembered hand, strangely without the regulation white glove, gently raised her. 'No, Miss Bannerman, it is I who must apologise. I thought to help by my intervention. I can see now that I misunderstood your situation.'

His kindness almost changed her mind about his arrogance. She had treated him shabbily, was pretending to be something she was not and she did not feel comfortable doing it. Scalding heat spread from her toes to her ears and she couldn't bear to look at him.

'You are distressed, my dear, I shall wait for you in the vestibule. Supper is about to be served, if I take you in that should serve to restore your reputation. Will you not look at me, Miss Bannerman?'

Slowly she met his gaze and saw nothing but sympathy there. 'I should not have run away but I am not comfortable in crowds, your Grace. I would much prefer to remain at home and read a book.' She glanced down at her hideous gown. 'My mama selected this; one might have thought she *wished* to make my evening a disaster.'

His brow creased for a second. Had she revealed too much of her real persona by her casual comment? Then his lips curved in the sweetest smile and for some reason she almost lost her balance. 'It is not a happy choice, my dear. I should have realized someone of your sensitivity would never appear in such a garment willingly.'

Good grief! He was agreeing she looked appalling. Surely a man of his breeding would realize his role was to reassure, not compound the problem? She would not spend another moment in his company. He *was* everything she most disliked in a gentleman — so full of his own importance that he thought he could say what he liked and it would give no offence. Her original opinion was entirely correct.

'I'm sorry but I do not feel well enough to eat. I'm going to remain in here until it's time to leave.' She should have thanked him for his kind offer, but the words remained unsaid. She whisked past him and into the retiring room before he could comment.

Several young ladies looked up from their toilette at her sudden entrance. She clapped her hands over her mouth as if about to cast up her accounts. She raced into the smaller chamber hoping they would think no more of her strange behaviour than that she had an attack of biliousness.

Rose remained where she was until she heard the door open and shut several times. She had been correct in her assumption and the original three occupants had returned to the activities. This was only one of several chambers set aside for the use of ladies during the long, tedious evening. A bevy of maids drifted in and out offering their services to stitch torn hems and re-pin elaborate *coiffeurs*.

Presently her sanctuary was interrupted by a helpful maid. 'Is there anything I can do to assist you, miss?'

'I am not feeling at all the thing. Is there anywhere I can sit quietly until my carriage arrives?'

The maid smiled sympathetically. 'Indeed there is. If you would care to come with me, I shall take you there. We often have young ladies needing to lie down; you will be nice and peaceful in there.'

Rose followed the girl through a communicating door and found herself in a large chamber in which there were several uncomfortable looking *chaise longues* and half a dozen upright chairs. Presumably the hostesses did not wish anyone to linger here from choice.

'Would it be possible to take a message to my sister, Miss Amelia Bannerman? I do not wish her to worry about my absence from the ballroom.'

'I shall send a footman directly, miss. Is there anything you would like? I could fetch you a cool drink.'

'Thank you, I need nothing except solitude.'

The girl curtsied and left. The room was decidedly chilly, the meagre fire not enough to warm the room. Rose should have asked for her cloak, she was going to be half dead with cold by the end of the evening. Picking up one of the chairs she carried it closer to the fire. At least there were sufficient candles to read without difficulty.

She was engrossed in her book when the maid re-appeared. 'Here, Miss Bannerman, I've brought your cloak.' The girl held up the item and her cheery smile and careful diction slipped. 'Mercy me, this ain't the right one. I beg your pardon, I'll fetch . . . '

'No, this is my sister's, but we are twins you know and share everything. It will do very well. I shall exchange it for my own later. Thank you so much for thinking of me, I shall be extremely comfortable now.' She held out a silver coin which was accepted gratefully. Thank goodness she'd had the forethought to bring some money with her.

Enveloped in the warm folds of Millie's cloak she settled down to read her novel. The title was 'Pride and Prejudice' and it was quite the best book she had ever encountered. There was something vaguely familiar about the characters, as if she had actually met them somewhere. No doubt this author based her characters on real

31

people which was why they seemed known to her.

★ ★ ★

Perry couldn't remain lurking in this corridor as it would draw more unwanted attention. He would promenade with his niece as promised and then retreat to his club. On reaching the ballroom he could not find his sister, but his eye was caught by another young lady laughing gaily as she was twirled around the floor.

If he was not mistaken the girl was Miss Amelia Bannerman. The fact that his rebuff had been unintentional and that Miss Bannerman's behaviour was caused by her timidity and lack of confidence, somehow made it worse. To be deliberately insulted would have been a novel experience. His lips twitched. Indeed, he could not remember ever meeting a person, male or female, who had had the courage to do so.

32

He strolled towards Amelia. Her eyes lit up when she saw him.

'Good heavens! You are the last person I expected to see here, your Grace. David told me you *never* come to Almack's.'

Perry smiled, his annoyance forgotten. Her sparkling wit enchanted him and he was attracted by her beauty. He bowed formally and she curtsied. 'This is the supper dance, Miss Bannerman. Would you do me the honour?'

She stepped in so her next remark would not be overheard by those all agog nearby. 'Sir, you do not have to dance with me if you do not wish to. I have stood up for every one and would be perfectly content to sit this one out.'

If he did not know better he would have thought she was in earnest rather than teasing him. With a flourish he placed her hand on his arm. 'Come, I shall endure for your sake.'

The intricacies of the dance, the constant to-ing and fro-ing, left little time for conversation and he heartily regretted his rash decision long before the music wailed to a halt. As he was leading his delightful partner into the supper room he came face-to-face with his sister. Her expression was comical.

'Lady Foster, allow me to introduce you to Miss Bannerman. Miss Bannerman, this is my sister.' The two ladies curtsied, but neither seemed inclined to prolong the conversation. 'We are going in to supper Laura, do you care to join us?'

Before Laura could answer, his companion giggled delightfully. 'I've been told the food is horrible. I shall not eat any of it, but I should be happy to sit with you, Lady Foster.'

'Thank you, Miss Bannerman, but I am returning to the ballroom.'

Something had seriously upset his normally even-tempered sibling. He was in for a bear garden jaw the next morning, that was the sure. A footman was waiting politely to speak to one of them. He raised his eyebrow.

'I beg your pardon, your Grace, but I

have a message for Miss Bannerman.'

Perry knew what this would be. He watched his partner's face turn from sunny to concerned. 'I must go at once, your Grace, my sister is unwell. I am so sorry to abandon you. You are far better going to your club if you wish to enjoy your supper.'

For the third time in one evening he was left to his own devices, but this time he was smiling. Had he finally found the woman he could bring himself to marry? Not only was Amelia Bannerman beautiful, she was witty and sweet natured. He would break the habit of a lifetime and call tomorrow in order to further his acquaintance.

★　★　★

Rose hid in the corner of the carriage hoping to divert her mother's torrent of disapproval by pretending to be asleep. The ploy failed. Mama was not deceived.

'Rosamond, your behaviour tonight was disgraceful. Not only did you destroy your own reputation you have possibly ruined your sister's chance of marrying the Duke of Essex.'

Millie patted her mother's hands. 'Please, Mama, don't upset yourself so, Rose has ruined nothing. Lord Bentley singled me out, that is enough to ensure I have a brilliant season.'

'If you put it like that, my love, then I am somewhat mollified. But this does not excuse your sister's appalling behaviour in front of the most important ladies of the *ton*.'

'If I had been obliged to wear that hideous gown I would have hidden in the retiring room as well. The idea was unfair of you, Mama. One might have thought you did not wish Rose to enjoy herself.'

'What an unkind thing to say to your mama, Amelia. I am deeply shocked by your suggestion. Did I not allow Rose to have lavender as she requested?'

Rose joined the conversation to defend herself. 'You did, but insisted on so many flounces and bows I looked ridiculous. I wanted a simple gown. With my figure and height it would have been much better so.'

'Rosamond, I shall take no criticism from you. You are in disgrace. You will not accompany your sister on any further outings until you have redeemed yourself.'

Glad the darkness hid her smile of delight, Rose settled back. 'Very well, Mama. I deserve to be confined to the house. I shall endeavour to behave myself if ever you relent and allow me to come out with you again.' She hoped her words sounded suitably contrite. Should she sniff, blow her nose a little? No, that would be doing it too brown. Instead, she dozed. Being excused the torture of overcrowded, stuffy ballrooms for the foreseeable future was a reward she had not anticipated. The embarrassment of being dressed up like a Guy tonight had been worthwhile. What a shame though that the man she'd carried in her heart all these years had proved to be nothing like the fantasy gentleman of her dreams. His image floated before her eyes. Yes, he was tall, had a striking countenance and filled his clothes to perfection, but this did not make up for his shortcomings. He was overbearing, dictatorial and stuffed full of pride.

An almost irresistible desire to giggle bubbled up. After all, if there was one man in the country entitled to think highly of himself then surely he was the one. Maybe she was being too hard on him; twice he had come to her rescue which showed another facet of his character. He was certainly a kind man when it suited him, but reconciling the two sides was all but impossible.

She kept her silence until safely in the apartment she shared with her sister.

'Millie, what did Mama mean? In what way could I have ruined your chances with the Duke?'

And so she heard with growing incredulity what had taken place after her retreat. For him to have danced was indeed a revelation.

'Did you like him, Millie?'

'I'm not sure, Rose. He's a charming gentleman and he listened to every word I said. But I must own to being puzzled by his reaction for I'm not famous for my wit, unlike you. I find him too formidable. He's not someone I could ever be comfortable with.'

'I should think not. You need a quite different sort of gentleman. You must not worry about it, dearest; I doubt very much you will be obliged to spend time with him again.'

'And you have what you wanted Rose, for in future you may remain at home. For my part though, I cannot tell you how much I enjoyed myself. I danced every dance and several of the gentlemen have promised to call tomorrow.'

'Is there any particular one you especially wish to see?'

'No one. I had hoped to find my true love tonight. I'm certain I should know him at once — our eyes would meet and that would be enough. But I shall not despair; tonight was my first appearance. I have dozens more invitations and I am bound to meet him before the end of the season, don't you think?'

Rose lost all desire to laugh. She had behaved deplorably, thinking only of herself. Had she not already decided the family needed *her* to replace the missing fortune? How could she do this if she was to remain at home? How could she persuade her mother to relent?

Soon the rhythmic breathing on the far side of the huge bed indicated her sister was asleep. Easing back the covers Rose slipped out and snatched up her thick dressing gown. The fire was still alight. At least their lack of funds had not reduced them to freezing cold bed chambers as yet. She curled up in her favourite chair to think the matter through. An hour later she was chilled to the marrow but had come up with a solution. She would convince Mama to allow her to attend the smaller gather-ings, the musical evenings and soirees. This was the sort of event where she was likely to meet a gentleman who would suit her requirements.

Millie would not be obliged to give up her dream of love. Her sister was not robust; being married for convenience would destroy her. *She* was made of sterner stuff, she had her books and her writing to lose herself in. Love was not something *she* needed to be content. Being the oldest, even if by only a few minutes, meant she must protect her younger sibling.

When she snuggled back under the covers she was obliged to grit her teeth to stop them chattering. Eventually warm enough to drift off to sleep, she closed her eyes, but for some extraordi-nary reason her dreams were full of the one man she wished to forget . . .

3

'I do hope you are not going to sit there scowling like that, Rosamond.'

'No, Mama, I'm going to retire to the window seat and keep my poor humour to myself.' Rose half-smiled. 'That's unless I have your permission to vanish entirely and thus avoid the necessity of watching Millie being fawned over by a small army of hopeful suitors.'

Her sister giggled but their mother pursed her lips. 'You may sit in the window seat, but you *will* greet any callers civilly. I wish to have no disappointing behaviour this afternoon, young lady.'

Quickly gathering up her novel, Rose retreated to the far end of the drawing-room. From here she could see the street below and warn her sister who to expect. The weather was inclement, but that was hardly surprising at the beginning of April. Maybe the blustery sleet would deter all but the most determined of young men from making a morning call. Their house was in the very centre of the metropolis, so most visitors could quite easily walk from their own homes and lodgings.

How ridiculous to have 'morning' calls in the afternoon — but that was society for you. She suspected most gentlemen and ladies did not rise until noon. Promptly at two o'clock the first young bucks arrived at the door. She recognized neither of them, so could not call out any information to Millie.

Her sister was dressed in a delightful velvet tea-gown in buttercup yellow and with her hair in studied disarray she looked quite lovely. Small wonder the two extremely youthful callers were hanging on her every word. Even the beady eye of their ever watchful mother could not deter them.

When the requisite one quarter of an hour was up, Mama rung her little brass bell and York, their decrepit butler, staggered in to escort the gentlemen out. So matters proceeded for the next forty-five minutes — a constant stream of hopeful visitors. Millie was right to have said her season was going to be a success. However none of the callers so far had passed muster with Mama or her sister.

At exactly three o'clock, the very last moment that could be considered polite to call, an imposing carriage rolled to a halt outside. To her surprise the Duke of Essex alighted. Her book tumbled to the floor.

'Millie, you'll never guess who has arrived. It's Lord Bentley . . . he's timed his visit to perfection. He will have you all to himself.'

Her mother gasped and fanned her cheeks with a periodical. Her sister paled and leaped to her feet in distress. 'Mama, I can't see him. I don't want him to court me. He's not the kind of man I could be happy with.'

Rose picked up her book and hurried over. 'Don't be a goose, my love. The Duke has come to pay his respects. A gentleman who danced with a young lady is expected to call the next day. This doesn't mean he's about to make you an offer.'

'Oh, I didn't realize . . . '

'Nonsense, Rosamond. I know for a fact Lord Bentley does not make morning calls.'

With a gurgle of laughter Rose shook her head. 'Mama, I hate to disagree, but as he is about to be announced, I know that he does.'

★ ★ ★

Today was to be a day for surprises. Perry had not expected such a substantial dwelling, or for the house to be in Grosvenor Square. Lord Bannerman was obviously a man of taste even if his business acumen was somewhat suspect.

He had not driven himself this afternoon because it would be dark by the time he completed his visit. The weather was too cold for him to travel in his recently purchased, high-perch phaeton. He climbed down and instructed his coachman: 'Walk the horses around the square, I shall not be above a quarter of an hour.'

The door was opened by a liveried footman. He had not needed to knock. He handed his beaver and gloves to the waiting minion and turned to the shrivelled butler. 'Lord Bentley to see . . . '

The old man nodded and, sucking on his single tooth, gestured towards the double doors that stood open across the elegant vestibule. The rumours he'd heard that the Bannerman household was in financial difficulties must be erroneous as there was a huge fire burning in the grate. This did not look to be a house forced to make economies.

Perry's lips twitched; he was obviously not to be announced but must find his own way in. The ancient retainer had already shambled back to his chair, positioned next to the heat. Perry was not accustomed to making morning calls. This was something he normally abhorred. However, one thing he did know was at this time he was likely to be the only visitor.

A rough looking footman bowed him in. 'Another gentleman caller, my lady,' he said loudly. There was the definite sound of laughter. Being considered a figure of fun was one thing that incensed Perry. He stepped in expecting to be bowled over by the beauty of Amelia but his attention was caught by her sister. Today she was wearing an elegant pink gown with a sash of a darker colour and this suited her to perfection. How could he have thought her plain last night? Her remarkable violet eyes were sparkling with laughter. This was the girl he had heard. His mouth tightened in annoyance.

* * *

Millie shifted closer. Rose slipped her arm unobtrusively around her sister's waist. When Symonds made his announcement she could not restrain her merriment. Where Papa found these strange men-servants she had no idea for they were certainly not in the common way. All desire to laugh, however, vanished as their visitor entered with every towering inch of him bristling with annoyance. She rose gracefully taking her sister with her. Their mother was also on her feet — this was a gentleman who demanded the utmost respect — and she addressed the Duke:

'I must apologise for the inadequacy of the staff; Symonds has yet to understand the niceties. You are welcome, your Grace.'

Millie was trembling and Rose bridled on her behalf. How dare this man frighten her sister by his disdainful glare? Nobody had asked him to call; this was his decision. *His* manners were lacking, not theirs. Gently moving her sister forward she tightened her hold and guided her into a synchronised curtsey. It took all her strength to bring Millie upright again without disaster. Their curmudgeonly visitor returned the salutation.

'Miss Bannerman, I have come to pay my respects as is required of me.'

Rose moved slowly back until she could feel the sofa hard against her legs. She sat, taking her shivering companion with her. Their mother resumed her seat and the Duke flicked aside his coat tails and folded his length onto the chair furthest away from the three of them.

An uneasy silence settled over the group. Mama, usually not short of conversation, was struck dumb by the importance of their caller. There was no point expecting Millie to speak. He would certainly not do so; it would be far beneath his dignity to initiate a conversation. Therefore Rose must remedy the situation. Quite forgetting she was supposed to be the timid and less intelligent of the two, she stiffened her spine and met him stare for stare.

'Lord Bentley, I must beg your pardon for . . . ' He raised an arrogant eyebrow and her desire to apologise was instantly replaced by something else entirely. She smiled sweetly and continued, ' . . . for refusing to dance with you yesterday. However, I am certain my sister made a far better partner. Her beauty would have matched the high opinion you have of yourself.'

Mama's hands flew up in shock and the Duke's mouth opened revealing two rows of even white teeth. Millie recoiled and buried her face in the high back of the sofa.

His mouth closed with a snap. Not only had she been unpardonably rude, she had also revealed her true character which would make her behaviour last night even more reprehensible. What had possessed her to speak so intemperately?

She was on her feet as he surged upwards. Instead of backing away from his anger she stepped closer, holding his gaze. 'I am so sorry, your Grace, that was unforgivable. You must realize I am the black sheep of the family. Normally I am kept locked in the attic where I can do no harm to anyone.'

His lips curved slightly and his rigid stance became less threatening. 'Might

I suggest, miss, that it would be advisable to remain incarcerated until you have . . . ' he tipped his head to one side, 'until you have acquired the same sweetness of disposition as your sister.' His dark blue eyes were dancing with laughter.

Millie and Mama did not see this was said in humour and they took his words as truth. Her sister, forgetting her nervousness, ran to confront the man who dared to suggest such a thing. Mama sailed across the carpet and stood protectively behind Rose. Lord Bentley, seeing he was surrounded, stifled his laughter and retreated to the far side of the room.

'Mama, Millie, his Grace did not mean it. It appears we both have an eccentric sense of fun.'

From a distance the gentleman in question added his confirmation. 'I can assure you, madam, my suggestion was made in jest. I do apologise if I upset you and Miss Amelia.'

As one the three of them swung

round to face him. He no longer resembled the haughty aristocrat he had been when he first stepped into the room; now he was a different person entirely. Someone charming and dangerously attractive.

Rose, for the first time, felt flustered in his presence. Her mother beamed at their guest, but Millie clapped her hands. 'My lord, I fear I did not understand the joke, but I'm delighted we are all friends again. Please, will you be seated?'

He shook his head and a lock of hair fell forward over one eye. A strange sensation fizzed around Rose's limbs. 'I have already outstayed my welcome. Lady Bannerman I came to ask your daughter to accompany me to the park at two o'clock tomorrow. Do I have your permission to escort her or will she be paying calls?'

Mama positively quivered with excitement. 'She will be here, your Grace, waiting when you drive up — it is far too inclement to keep your team standing.'

With a formal nod he took his leave

and the room seemed empty afterwards. Rose drifted back to the window seat. The light of the lanterns made it just possible to see him climb into his carriage. She sighed. He was definitely interested in Millie but he was quite wrong for her sister. She would make it her business to discourage his intentions.

★ ★ ★

That evening Rose ate her supper alone in the private parlour attached to her shared bed chamber. Millie had gone to Lady Charlotte Simpson's come out ball. Rose had promised to remain awake until her sister returned so she could be told every detail. She was well pleased with the arrangement they had come to — her mother had agreed Rose could attend lesser events and she was to go out the following night to an intimate gathering to hear a much lauded soprano sing. It had also been understood between them that she could adjust her wardrobe as she saw fit. Both she and Mary, her abigail, had been busy all evening removing frills and furbelows from all her formal evening wear.

But the hour was now late, and Mary had been dismissed long ago. The clock showed an hour after midnight when Rose heard the first carriages returning. Millie would be home very soon and she was to act as her maid tonight. Carefully hanging up the garment she had been working on, she picked up the warming pan and ran it several times through the bed. Satisfied the sheets were no longer icy and that everything was ready, she returned to her seat by the fire.

Less than twenty minutes later running footsteps heralded Millie's arrival. Rose's heart thumped uncomfortably. Something untoward had occurred for nothing else could account for this unaccustomed speed. She stood up and waited, her fingers entwined, dreading what disaster might have befallen whilst she had not been at Millie's side to protect her.

The door burst open and her sister flung herself across the room to grasp Rose's hands. 'You will never guess what happened tonight. I have met him again. Things happened exactly as I thought they would. One glance was all it took between us to know that we are destined to be together.'

'Who is the lucky man? Is he someone suitable?'

Millie twirled around the room, her domino flying out in a cloud of saffron silk. 'Do you recall that summer five years ago when you persuaded me to climb a tree and I fell out?' Rose nodded, guessing what would follow. 'Well, Sir Richard Devonshire is the gentleman who caught me and he is the man I have fallen in love with.'

'From what I remember he's certainly a personable young man. I believe he's still David's friend, and our brother is a good judge of character.'

Her sister flopped into a chair. 'Richard is everything I ever dreamt of for a husband. He's perfect in every way. Although not as rich as some others we know, he is well able to take care of me. He is coming tomorrow at two o'clock to speak to Mama.'

Good grief! This young man was as impetuous and impractical as her sister. They had neither of them thought the matter through. To become betrothed after one meeting — two if you counted the summer all those years ago — was unlikely to meet with approval from either family. But Millie was so happy that Rose couldn't bear to spoil things for her.

'I suggest, dearest, that you do not speak of your feelings to Mama just yet. She will fly into high alt and write to our papa and we do not wish him to be worried at this time, do we?'

'Very well, I will do as you suggest. But if I am asked, then I shall not lie.'

Rose carefully removed her sister's finery and tossed it over the wooden stand. They scrambled into bed and, as usual, her sister was soon in the land of nod, without a thought to the problem that now occurred to Rose: Millie was already committed to driving with Lord Bentley at two o'clock the following day, and her sister could not be in two places at once. Rose must come up with a satisfactory solution.

Well — the request had been that 'a daughter' accompany him. As he had not specified which of them he was referring to, he could not cavil if *she* appeared in her sister's place. With luck he would arrive on the hour and they would be gone before Sir Richard arrived. Heaven knows what their mother's reaction would be when this gentleman appeared and she discovered Millie was not the one who had left with the Duke.

* * *

Millie was more than happy to fall in with this scheme. She hated to deceive their mama but agreed there was no other way. So it was that Millie sat flicking through the pages of the latest *La Belle*

57

Assemblée, whilst Rose stood in the huge closet viewing her many outfits.

'Mary, I must find something comparable to an ensemble Millie would wear. If I look too dissimilar I'll be recognized and the Duke might well refuse to take me up.'

'It's not for me to say, miss, but I think you're asking for trouble. His Grace will be right cross with you both. I don't reckon he's a gentleman used to being tricked.'

Rose did not reprimand her for the comment. Mary had been taking care of them for so long she felt entitled to voice her opinions in this way

'I'm sure you are correct, however I have no choice. Millie wouldn't be happy with him, he frightens her.'

Her eye alighted on an outfit ordered for her sister that had been made, in error, to fit herself. This was in royal blue — not a favourite colour of hers — and liberally festooned with unnecessary gold decoration. It had never been worn.

'Excellent. I shall wear this; I seem to remember it has a bonnet with an extremely wide brim. It will be all but impossible for him to see my face.'

Decked out in the gaudy gown and matching pelisse, the ridiculous bonnet on her head, she stepped into the sitting room. The magazine fell from Millie's fingers. 'Oh! I had forgotten about that outfit. Royal blue and gold is rather startling, is it not?'

Rose could think of several less flattering descriptions.

'It is certainly not an ensemble one is likely to forget. I cannot think what possessed you to insist on so much frogging everywhere. I thank the good Lord at least my own half-kid boots are plain.'

Giggling, Millie ran to embrace her. 'At least no one shall recognize you inside that bonnet. To tell you the truth, I'm relieved I never had to wear that outfit. I shall never forget your kindness, darling Rose, and would do the same for you.'

Mary, who was watching from the

window, called out. 'My goodness, would you look at that! He's bought one of them high up carriages. You wouldn't get me on one of those, I can tell you.'

'Thank goodness I am not going out with him; I would have been terrified to sit so far above the ground. Good luck, Rose.'

Rose timed her exit to perfection. She whisked through the vestibule in a flurry of royal blue and gold whilst Millie, from the stairs, called her farewells to their mama, who was in the drawing-room. The front door was open. She ran lightly down the steps keeping her head lowered. As she had hoped the Duke had remained aloft leaving his tiger, and a footman, to assist her into the vehicle.

'Good afternoon, Miss Bannerman, it is fortunate the sun is out as it will make the drive so much more pleasant.' Solicitously he tucked the rug around her knees, snapped his whip expertly, flicked the reins and the phaeton moved smoothly into the road.

4

Whilst the Duke was concentrating on his driving there was less likelihood of him becoming aware of the deception. What would he do if he discovered he was taking the wrong sister for a drive in the park before they had left the confines of the square? From under the brim of her bonnet Rose spotted Sir Richard heading for the house. As the brim of his hat was pulled down low and he was wearing a muffler around his neck, she sincerely hoped he would remain unrecognized by the gentleman beside her. The Duke was no fool. Before long he would realize he had been fobbed off with the wrong sister, but as long as he thought it a harmless prank she was sure he would not be unduly dismayed. Discovering he had been snubbed for a lesser mortal would be another matter entirely.

From her lofty perch she was able to see the gates of the park long before they arrived. If she was honest, she was enjoying the experience. The Duke was an excellent whip and handled his spirited team of matching black thoroughbreds with authority. He was obliged to join a queue of like-minded vehicles wishing to enter.

'Miss Bannerman, I do hope you're not cold. I can assure you once we have the protection of the trees you will find it less windy.'

Swallowing a lump that had unaccountably appeared in her throat, she tried to think of something to say that would not instantly reveal who she was. 'We are very high up, your Grace.'

'We are indeed, and I fear we will remain so even when we are in the park.'

Rose turned her head sharply to see him barely restraining his mirth.

'You have known all along that I replaced my sister, have you not?'

'I am not in my dotage, my dear girl.

My eyes are working as well as they should. Even dressed in that extraordinary outfit I was well aware of your identity. You are half a head taller and move quite differently to your sister.'

'I suppose I should apologise, but I don't intend to. If you hadn't wished to take me up you could have said so when I came out, so I must assume you are happy with the arrangement.'

'Intrigued would be more accurate. Would you care to explain why you and your sister felt obliged to attempt to bamboozle me? Why should driving in the park with me be considered unacceptable?'

'My sister had toothache so I volunteered to take her place.' This sounded a lame excuse even to her own ears.

He remained silent as he guided the team through the gates. Inside, the park was teeming with similar couples, some in open carriages, others promenading on foot. As this was her first season she had not been escorted anywhere and was quite unused to the many knowing nods and smiles that were being directed at her. She shrank back into her bonnet, wishing she were anywhere but so prominently displayed in the most ridiculous and outdated costume.

'Well, my dear, it will not do for you to cower against the seat. You wished to accompany me to this public a place and you must do your best to enjoy the experience.'

This was to be her punishment; he wished to embarrass her in front of his friends. She had not thought it through, as usual, and now she was getting her comeuppance. She hated his patronising voice, hated him for subjecting her to such humiliation. He would not come out of this escapade unscathed if she had anything to do with it.

Sitting straight, she turned to him and fluttered her eyes. 'Your Grace,' she simpered, 'for a moment the significance of being accompanied by someone so extremely illustrious quite overcame me.'

His demeanour changed; he was no

longer smiling. 'Miss Bannerman, before you embark on something you will regret, let me remind you it would be unwise to make an enemy of me.'

This threat had the opposite effect. Before he could take evasive action she slid along the box until she was pressed hard against his side then she deliberately turned her head so that he was trapped within the brim of her bonnet. To anyone observing it would seem as if he was kissing her. He was famous for his avoidance of entanglements so to be seen with a young lady so gaudily dressed should puncture his pomposity. Her gesture was over in a moment, but she had seen the fury in his eyes and was already regretting her childish manoeuvre. It was too late now though to worry about the possible consequences. Her impulsive determination to put him in his place, to make *him* look ridiculous, had surely been a success judging by the gaping and gawping of those in their vicinity. But instead of reprimanding her or giving her one of his famous set downs, he clicked his tongue and urged his team into a spanking trot. Within moments they were in a deserted part of the park. He drove his team into a clearing and reined in. If it had not been so high from the ground Rose would have jumped out.

'What were you thinking of? Don't you realize what you have just done, you stupid girl?'

Even his rudeness did not rouse her. He was entitled to berate her, she had behaved appallingly. What was it about this man brought out the very worst in her?

'Well? Have you nothing to say for yourself?' Dumbly she shook her head. There was nothing she could say that would improve matters between them.

'Look at me, young lady, I have no wish to talk to your bonnet.'

Reluctantly Rose twisted on the seat and raised her head. Instead of seeing anger she saw regret. Confused, she started to apologise.

'I did not think . . . I should not have done it.'

'You still don't realize the enormity of your action, do you?' He was talking to her as if she was a simpleton. 'We apparently exchanged a kiss in the most public place in London. I can do one of two things, both equally repellent to me.'

Her eyes widened at his tone.

'I should like you to take me home. I'm sure no one will have recognized me for I have not been seen in society apart from the other night. All the damage that has been done is to your . . . '

He interrupted. 'You are right. No one will have recognized *you* as my companion. They will have deduced they were seeing your sister behaving disgracefully. You have effectively ruined her reputation.'

This could not be true. How could something so harmless have done such dreadful damage? She closed her eyes trying to digest this unpalatable truth.

He was quite right of course. One did not embrace in public at all, and for an unmarried girl to do so was indeed the end of her good name. Unless . . . is that what he meant by having to do something repellent?

'I see you have finally understood what you have done. I must marry your sister or tarnish her good name for ever. Which do you think I should do?'

His bland tone incensed her.

'You do not have to do either.' Without a second thought she untied the bow at her neck and tossed the bonnet high up into the trees. 'I don't believe there could be any mistake about your companion now; my sister is well known for having golden curls.'

'The devil take it! You're quite impossible. It's high time someone took you in hand and I believe you have just given me permission to do so.'

'I have done no such thing. My reputation is already in tatters after my exhibition at Almack's. I can assure you I should be delighted to retire to the country in disgrace.'

He looked at her through narrowed eyes. 'But, child, I should not. Whatever your feelings on the matter might be, consider yourself engaged to me.'

He must be touched in the attic to say such a thing.

'I shall not. You might be the most eligible party in the world for all I care. I do not like you and have absolutely no intention of marrying you.' She glared at him, daring him to disagree. To her utter astonishment he threw back his head and roared with laughter.

Unfortunately during their conversation his attention had not been on his cattle. The reins had become slack in his fingers and his sudden shout threw them into a panic. They took off, bits between their teeth, and Rose was obliged to cling on for dear life whilst the Duke fought for control.

The matter was never in any doubt. Within a short space of time he had his team calmed and he trotted them for a further half a mile until they were cool.

Only then did he glance over to see how she did. Rose was quite put out. For all he knew she could have tumbled over the side and broken her neck, the amount of attention he had paid her.

'Still here? I hoped to have dislodged you and by your demise have solved my problem.'

Her annoyance vanished. 'How strange you should have spoken my thoughts exactly, your Grace.'

'You didn't think to throw yourself over the side in a dramatic suicidal gesture?' His grin disarmed her.

'I considered it, but discarded the idea. I don't wish to cause my family any more upset than I already have.'

For a moment he seemed disconcerted, as if believing her reply to be serious, then he chuckled.

'You are an original. It will certainly not be dull married to you.'

'Your Grace, please do not continue to tease me. You have no more intention of marrying *me* than I do of marrying my butler. There must be another way out of this muddle.'

'If you had not discarded your bonnet it might have been possible for me to marry your sister instead.' His tone became even, his eyes hard. 'I can assure you I would have much preferred that alternative. But whatever your feelings on the matter, your behaviour today has given us no option. It will be a marriage of convenience. Do not expect me to pretend to hold you in high regard.'

Rose shrivelled under his inspection and blinked away her tears. She would never show him how much his words had hurt. It had been her intention to sacrifice herself on the altar of matrimony for her family, but never in her worst nightmares had she considered she would be obliged to marry *this* man. To marry another without love would have been tolerable. To marry him, feeling as she did and knowing he despised her, was unbearable.

★ ★ ★

Perry regretted his harsh words. She was little more than a child and had done what she did out of mischief not design. Her escapade would be all over town by this evening. In order to protect her he had no choice. His sister had been telling him this past year he should be thinking of entering parson's mousetrap. So be it. He had no time for love and all that flummery. He might as well marry this girl as any other. Her breeding was impeccable, she was certainly a lively companion . . . but she was not the wife he had envisaged for himself.

He glanced sideways at her. She had drawn herself upright, her chin thrust out in defiance. He could not fault her courage; he just wished he could bring himself to at least feel affection for her. This situation was going to be difficult for both of them, but so much harder for her. He must remember she was barely out of the schoolroom and could not be more than eighteen years of age. The least he could do was put it about that this was a love match. He would say that when he had rescued her from the tree five years ago he had decided she was the one for him.

★ ★ ★

The drive back was interminable, and Rose was certain he was as relieved as she to reach Grosvenor Square. The diminutive groom raced to the horses' heads and held them. She waited until a footman arrived to assist her to dismount. She could not bring herself to look at him; she had ruined both their lives by her stupidity. No wonder he hated her, for she hated herself.

'My dear, I shall return in two hours to speak to your mother. We must convince everyone we are besotted, nothing else will do. When does your father arrive from India?'

'He should be back by the end of May. The last letter we received informed us that he was about to set sail. David returns with him.'

'Excellent. I can draw up the settlements then. I'm sure you do not wish to be married until he has returned. We will be married in September, which should give you ample time to put together your bride clothes.'

Too dispirited to argue, Rose nodded and descended, with the assistance of Symonds, to the path. Without a backward glance she hurried in. She must change into her own clothes before she went to see her mother. Only then did she recall Mama would already know of the deception. She prayed that Millie's afternoon had passed better than hers. She paused at the door; what if there were still visitors?

'Symonds, is anyone with my mother in the drawing-room?'

'No, there were only the one today. Lady Bannerman has gone out a-visiting, and Miss Amelia went with her.'

Upstairs, Mary greeted her with exclamations of dismay. 'Lawks, miss, just look at the state of you! You look as if you've been through a hedge backwards.'

'Please, Mary, help me to disrobe. Lord Bentley will be returning shortly to speak to my mother. I wish to take a bath and put on the new gown that arrived last week.'

Her maid was bursting with curiosity but had more sense than to enquire. Rose prayed her mama and Millie would have returned before the expected visit. She must explain to her sister the real circumstances; she was prepared to dissemble with her parents but not with her twin.

Attired in her most becoming ensemble with her hair loosely arranged on her crown and threaded with violet ribbons, she believed she looked her best. Her gown was a delicate shade of mauve but what made it special were the tiny violets embroidered on the hem, the cuffs and around the neckline. Her necklace, two rows of amethysts, enhanced the whole.

Millie arrived in the bed chamber as she was preparing to leave. 'Goodness, Rose, you look quite breath-taking. I love the way your hair has been arranged. Why have you gone to so much trouble?'

By the time it had all been explained Millie was wringing her hands in despair. 'You cannot go through with this. I shall not let you. This is all my fault.'

'Do you wish to marry your Richard?'

'I do. He came with us when we went on our morning call to the Simpsons. Charlotte was beside herself for I believe she had designs on him herself.' Millie clapped her hands. 'Mama is quite resigned to my choice and thought our deception romantic.'

'In which case, I shall willingly go ahead with this arrangement. If I'm to marry Lord Bentley, and save the family from ruin, then you are free to marry Richard. And if I have to marry for convenience, I would much prefer to be a duchess,' Rose replied with feigned insouciance. The fact that her prospective husband cordially disliked her and also believed her singly unattractive was something she would not share, even with her dearest Millie.

* ★ *

Mama looked up from her magazine. 'Well, Rose, did the Duke give you a severe set down for impersonating your sister?'

'No, Mama, not really. In fact I have surprising news for you. We are engaged. Lord Bentley is coming to speak to you at any moment.'

The periodical fell to the floor. 'My dear Rose, you are funning me. It is ever your way to make a jest of things.' Her mama shook her head.

Rose's heart fell. If her own Mama thought it a mismatch, an aberration, then how could they hope to convince the *ton*? Then she recalled her mother had never heard the story of the oak tree. She regaled her parent, liberally embellishing it with romance, and by the time her tale had ended her mother was more sanguine. Believing this fabrication was surely not so difficult; after all she *had* been infatuated with him these past five years. How silly she had been with her childish fantasies.

'You sly puss, no wonder you have no wish to attend any balls. You were just waiting for him to come and make his offer. Though I can hardly believe that a Duke has loved you since you were in the schoolroom. Now, if you were to tell me he had secretly loved your sister all these years, I could readily understand it. After all *she* is the beauty of the family, and her nature is as delightful as her appearance.' She pursed her lips and looked hard at Rose. 'However, I can't condone your outlandish behaviour these past few days. You would not have done these things if your papa had been at home.'

This conversation was brought to an abrupt halt when Symonds flung open the drawing-room door and announced in a voice that would have done service on a parade ground, 'The Duke of Essex here to see you, my lady.'

5

Rose gripped the back of the chair as her mother sailed forward to greet their visitor with more than necessary enthusiasm. 'Your Grace, I am delighted to welcome you. In future you must not stand on ceremony, but call whenever you wish.' She stared rather pointedly at Rose who slowly emerged from behind her support. 'I cannot tell you how surprised I am to see you here and on such an errand. As I said to my daughter earlier, if it had been Amelia you had been pining for I could have understood it better.'

Rose flinched and hid her embarrassment in a neat curtsy. He reached down and raised her. She was inexorably drawn to him; if she had not known the truth she would have thought him genuinely fond of her.

'My dear, I must speak to your

mother alone for a few moments. Is there somewhere you can wait for me to join you?'

Her mother answered for her. 'Go to the yellow sitting-room, my love, there is a fire lit.'

He gently pressed her hand and then released it. She curtsied again and all but ran from the room. Her cheeks were scarlet; keeping up this pretence was going to be far more difficult than she'd anticipated, especially when everybody would be saying the same. Hopefully they would not, like Mama had, say it in her presence.

* * *

Perry wished he could make things easier for her, but this tangle was of her own doing and it would do her no harm to suffer a little embarrassment. Society knew both girls were in the marriage mart to find a wealthy husband. Rosamond had trapped him neatly; if he did not know better he might have thought it done deliberately.

'Lady Bannerman, in the absence of your husband, I'm obliged to ask your permission to pay my addresses to your daughter. I shall leave the matter of settlements until Lord Bannerman is returned to this country. I understand he has already set sail from India.'

'He has indeed, your Grace. I'm sure he will be as delighted as I am that Rosamond has secured such an advantageous match. I did not expect she would take for she has always been headstrong and forever leading dear Amelia into countless scrapes. But her papa always favoured Rosamond and he would not curb her high spirits.'

'Her lively nature attracted me. And I can assure you, madam, I find her appearance as pleasing as her sister's. I think she looks quite ravishing in the gown she now has on.' He could think of nothing else to say to praise the young woman he was supposed to be in love with. Then an image of her face, of her remarkable eyes floated before him.

'I can safely say that she has the finest eyes of any woman in London. If you will excuse me, ma'am, I am eager to join your daughter.'

'Of course. We are going to a musicale at the Leadbetter's in Brook Street this evening, I do hope you will accompany us.'

The last thing he wanted to do was dance attendance on the girl's family, but he was now obligated to escort them until Lord Bannerman or David returned to do it in his stead. 'Unfortunately, Lady Bannerman, I have a prior engagement. However, I shall be at your service tomorrow evening. I expect you will also be going to the come out ball of Lady Isobel Ponsonby. Do you wish me to send my carriage to collect you?'

'So kind, but we will make our own way there. It is nonsense for you to come even such a short distance out of your way when the weather is so poor. However, shall we agree to meet at nine o'clock at the venue?'

This was the first sensible thing the woman had said. 'I shall look forward to it,' he replied gratefully. With a final nod he strode off to find Rosamond and make her a formal offer. He had already collected from the bank the priceless heirloom always given as a betrothal ring to a future duchess. It grieved him to be handing it over to such an undisciplined girl, but he was hopeful that, with firm guidance, he could mould her in a way that would better reflect the importance of his family.

★ ★ ★

Rose paced the room, racking her brains for a way she could extricate herself from this unhappy arrangement. From whichever direction she looked at it, marriage to the Duke would be an unmitigated disaster for both of them. She was not his ideal duchess and they would constantly be at loggerheads. It was not in her nature to hold her tongue when she had something she thought worth saying.

She had deliberately left the door open so the extra light from the oriel window opposite would brighten the room. Firm footsteps echoed in the passage way. He would be here in a moment and she was no nearer a solution. Collapsing onto the nearest chair, she folded her skirts neatly about her ankles and placed her hands demurely in her lap. She tried to steady her breathing; her heart was pounding so loud she was all but deafened.

He paused in the doorway, blocking the light. She could not help thinking this sudden darkness was an omen. Framed as he was, he certainly looked devilish. He was dressed in a dark-blue superfine coat, beige breeches and black Hessians. The snowy white cravat frothing at his neck did little to alleviate the overall impression. Even his features were dark, his hair black as soot and his eyes matching his topcoat. Her heart quailed; he was too much for her.

Whatever he wanted she knew she would have no option but to obey. He was born to command. What chance did a mere girl have against one so powerful?

'I have spoken to your mother and she has given me permission to address you.'

She was so dispirited she did not bother to pretend she was any happier with the arrangement than he was.

'Did you expect her to do otherwise? There's not a mama in the country who would not welcome you with open arms. You are a Duke, and fabulously wealthy. Not only that, you are reasonably personable and still quite young. No doubt every young lady's Prince Charming.'

He entered, bringing the light with him. She waited for him to show his anger at her impertinence, but to her surprise he strolled across the room and picked up an upright chair. Holding it by two fingers as if it weighed nothing at all, he spun the chair and straddled it. He folded his arms across the back, steepled his fingers and rested his chin on them.

'Thank you for your honesty. I gather that you do not share the opinion of *every young lady?*'

'As you appear to value the truth, I shall tell you I am appalled that a moment's stupidity on my part has brought us to this. We both deserve better than to be shackled to each other in a loveless marriage.'

'Are you quite sure you are only approaching your eighteenth name day? You have a mature head on your young shoulders. I know it's going to be difficult, but surely not impossible?' He stared at her. She was mesmerised. 'I don't believe any Bentley has married for love. As far as I know none of the relationships were any the worse for that.'

'That's as may be. As long as you're quite clear I've only agreed to marry you in order to save the family's fortunes and so Millie can marry

Richard Devonshire. She would have been an even worse choice than me as your bride. At least I am capable of standing up for myself if I have to.'

'My dear, your desire to help your family is laudable. However, I can assure you the only reason we are to marry is because we have no other option. I am a gentleman. Whatever you might think of me, I could not stand by and see your name in shreds. I don't think you realize your whole family would be tarnished by your disgrace. I doubt even someone as amiable as Richard would wish to ally himself to a Bannerman if that was the case.'

'Then I suppose I must thank you for your gallantry. Society is a harsh taskmaster, don't you think? We are both to be sacrificed on the altar of etiquette, and I shall always regret what I have done.' She looked up with tear-filled eyes. 'I shall do my best to be a good wife to you, to try and make up for ruining your life.'

'Then it shall not be so bad — for

either of us. Now, little one, there's something I've yet to do.'

The formal offer — she would feel better once that had been said. But the words she expected were not spoken; instead he reached across and placed a small velvet box in her hand. She stared at it. This was too much. No offer and a betrothal ring she must place upon her own finger? He could not have made it clearer; he was fulfilling his obligations but felt not even a glimmer of affection.

She dropped the box on the carpet and scrambled to her feet. She must get away. She would not break down in front of him. She was almost at the door when his arms encircled her. Without a by-your-leave she was swept up and carried to the *chaise-longue* to the right of the fire. She buried her wet cheek in his shoulder for she was too miserable to struggle.

In one smooth movement he arranged himself keeping her cradled on his lap. She must protest, get free from him, but somehow she felt safe resting there. His hand was stroking her hair and he was murmuring. 'Come, sweetheart, you must not cry. I know this betrothal is not to your liking, no more it is mine. But we shall make the best of it. Who knows, in time we might feel quite differently.'

A soft white square was placed in her fingers. His kindness was even harder to accept than his indifference. She gulped, swallowed and blew her nose noisily. She shouldn't be sitting on his lap. Such a thing was quite improper even if they were now engaged. She raised her face in order to ask to be released but the intensity of his gaze left her incapable of speech. His eyes darkened and one hand cupped her face. He was no more than a hand's breadth from her.

★ ★ ★

He couldn't help himself. His lips gently touched each damp eye in turn; he tasted the salt of her tears and something twisted inside him. From nowhere he felt an overwhelming urge to protect this girl, to somehow make things right for her.

What happened was inevitable. His mouth trailed kisses across her cheek and then he found her lips with his own. He had not intended to make love to her. Until that moment this had been the last thing on his mind. But having her resting warm and heavy on his lap and seeing her tear-streaked face, he was unable to resist.

He increased the pressure and to his delight she responded. She came alive in his arms and changed in that instant from a girl to a woman grown.

* * *

Languor slowly spread throughout her limbs. Rose wanted the kiss to go on forever. She pressed against him and her hands, of their own volition, buried themselves in the thick hair at the base of his skull.

Abruptly she was set aside and he

was standing with his back to her. Had she offended him by her unmaidenly response? Had she to apologise yet again for her behaviour? Her eyes filled. Her pleasure in the embrace vanished.

She pushed herself upright and retreated to the window.

★   ★   ★

Damn it to hell. This wasn't supposed to happen. He couldn't turn until his arousal subsided. What must she think of him?

Keeping his coattails across the embarrassment he turned to face her. Rose was standing by the window, her face pale. 'I beg your pardon. I took shameful advantage of you. I give you my word I will not importune you in that way again.'

Her expression was frosty. 'I understood our relationship was to be . . . to be a convenient one. I have no wish for a repeat of such intimacies.'

He nodded. 'I apologise again.

Perhaps we can . . . '

She turned her back on him. The
velvet box lay on the carpet. He had
made a sad mull of things. Better to
leave now and return to mend fences
tomorrow. He scooped up the ring and
shoved it back into his waistcoat pocket.
'I bid you good day, Miss Bannerman.'
He got no response.

* * *

He could not have made his feelings
plainer; no formal offer and no
betrothal ring. Rose curled up on the
window seat burying her head in her
knees. She would not cry again, she had
shed enough tears for that man already
today. She must return to the safety of
her apartment before her mother came
to congratulate her on her success. As
it happened, Millie had developed a
megrim so Rose spent the afternoon
comforting her. Millie was too unwell
to go to the musicale, where she had
planned to meet Richard, so was tearful

as well as poorly.

'Dearest, you must not upset yourself. You have the rest of the season to enjoy outings with your beloved. To miss one evening is a mere bagatelle.'

'I did so want to tell him about your engagement. He would know immediately this news means he's free to offer for me.'

'You have only just met him, ninny, you should not be thinking of receiving an offer so soon.'

Her sister raised her head from the pillow. 'You are engaged already and you do not even love Lord Bentley.'

'I had no choice, you know that. And you must promise not to tell anyone our feelings are not involved. I have no wish to damage his reputation further. After all, isn't that what he values most?'

★ ★ ★

Rose got up early as usual to take her morning ride. Mary had left her riding clothes neatly arranged in the dressing room. It took a matter of minutes to put them on and push her feet into her riding boots. At their country estate she was allowed to ride astride so always wore a divided skirt with her habit.

She loved the house when quiet with only the servants scrubbing floors and dusting furniture to disturb the peace. The stable yard, even so early, was already busy. Orion, her pretty grey, greeted her enthusiastically.

'Perfect morning for a ride, miss; reckon you'll be able to get a bit of a gallop in today.'

'I hope so, Tom. It's been far too long since the ground was soft enough.' She turned and offered him her bent leg. He tossed her into the saddle. She rammed her boot into the single stirrup iron and gathered up the reins. Her groom mounted his gelding and they were ready to depart.

Suddenly Orion threw up her head and skittered sideways as a huge black stallion trotted in through the archway.

'Good morning, my love, I do hope I have not kept you waiting.'

Rose closed her mouth and settled her horse. 'No, your Grace, you are not tardy. That's a magnificent animal. I wonder if my mare will have difficulty keeping up.'

'Never fear, I shall match my pace to yours.'

They clattered out of the yard together, Tom a respectful distance behind them. Only the road sweepers and servants hurrying on errands for their masters and mistresses were about so early in the day. Her mare danced over the cobbles, frequently swinging her hindquarters in towards the massive beast beside her.

'It would seem, your Grace, my horse has taken a fancy to your stallion. What do you call him?'

'Lucifer. Don't raise your eyebrows, my dear, the name was not my choice. He arrived at my stud with it and will answer to none other.'

The Duke was all but irresistible

when in this teasing mood. Should she forget his unkindness yesterday and begin to hope again?

In no time at all they were in the park and, as expected, the place was empty. She urged Orion into a canter and seeing no other riders ahead of her she clicked her tongue. All her worries and disappointments blew away with the sheer joy of galloping flat-out. Her mare was not tall but famous for her fleetness and no animal had ever matched her speed. Then she was aware the Duke was about to overtake, the black nose of his stallion drawing closer. She crouched in the saddle. Orion responded magnificently. For a few minutes she maintained her lead then he was riding parallel and the race was over.

Laughing, her hair in disarray and her cap long gone, Rose transferred her weight to the back of the saddle and gently pulled the reins. Her mare obediently dropped from a gallop to pay canter and then to a smooth walk. She turned to smile at her companion.

'Lucifer is the first to catch us up. Can you imagine how fast any progeny of these two might be?'

'My thoughts exactly. Has your mare ever been in a foal?'

'No, she is five this summer, a perfect age. I had hoped to find a suitable sire in the country but it would seem the matter has been solved for me.'

'When we are married in the autumn we can turn them out together and let nature take its course.'

Tom trotted up to meet them her lost cap in his hand. 'Thank you, Tom. This is not the first time my groom has been obliged to find my headgear. For some reason, no matter how many pins I put in, it always finds a way to escape.'

The Duke chuckled. 'If you travelled at a more decorous speed, my love, I'm certain you would not have this problem. Now, the horses are cool, shall we canter back to the gates?'

6

Rose was content to walk through the busier streets with the massive bulk of Lucifer on her right, her groom directly behind her. Tonight they were to attend the Ponsonby ball together and there was a point on which she needed to reassure the Duke.

'Lord Bentley, you will be relieved to hear I have removed all decoration from my ball gown. It is not an outstanding ensemble, but it will do.'

He surveyed her from top to toe, bringing colour to her cheeks. 'I think we might do better than that. It would not do for the Duke of Essex to appear with his betrothed in anything but the height of fashion.'

'Are you now to have control over my wardrobe as well as my life?'

'I have extremely deep pockets, my dear girl. Allow me to indulge myself by spending my blunt on my future wife. I promise I shall send you something suitable by this afternoon.' He smiled at her expression. 'Tomorrow a top modiste shall visit you; order whatever you like. A tall girl like you will dress to advantage.'

She was not sure if she was offended or thrilled by his offer to clothe her, but she had to refuse. 'I thank you for your kindness, sir, but don't you see? I cannot be decked out in the very best when my sister and mama must make do with what we have already purchased.'

'Did I not say? Of course your sibling and your mother must replenish their wardrobes as well. I suggest that, until *you* have your new gowns, you refuse invitations.'

'Have you not heard the well-known saying, your Grace, that beauty is in the eye of the beholder? If you are ashamed to be seen with me as I am then I shall, in future, only attend events at which you will not be. I bid you good morning.'

She dug her heel into the mare's side and cantered off. Grosvenor Square was the next turning. She whisked through the archway and into the stable yard before he had time to react. Kicking her boot from the stirrup and unhooking her knee from the pommel, she dropped lightly to the cobbles. A waiting stable boy took the reins and she raced for the side door. Not a moment too soon. She heard him call her name but ignored him and headed for her apartment. Even he would not presume to accost her there.

Millie was still asleep. After a sick headache her twin would often remain in bed until luncheon the following day. Mary, well used to her mistress's morning activities, was waiting with hot water and fresh garments.

Rose did not mention to her mama the Duke intended to re-clothe them all. Time enough for that if it actually happened. Several times during the day she felt her mother's eyes upon her, but nothing was said so she thought perhaps she was oversensitive. There were no callers and, most unusually, Mama did not go out to visit friends.

Her sister appeared in time for afternoon tea, a trifle pale but otherwise fully recovered. Mama was in the process of pouring the first cup when Symonds stomped in, a large parcel in his arms. 'Couldn't knock and carry at the same time, my lady. This here has arrived for Miss Bannerman.'

His sudden entrance caused her mother's hand to jerk and tea dropped on to the priceless carpet. A full quarter of an hour passed before order was restored, the stain removed by a diligent parlour maid, and fresh tea ready.

'My word, whatever can be in that box? Rose, aren't you going to open it?'

'I believe I know what's inside. Lord Bentley said he would send me something more appropriate to wear for tonight's event. I do not want it and shall not wear it, so there's little point in looking.'

Millie fell on the box. 'In which case,

I shall open it for you. Imagine, you have only been engaged since yesterday and already he is sending you presents.'

Soon the room was full of tissue. Rose tried to look disinterested but was in truth as eager as her sister and mother to see what was in the box. Millie was staring down at the content with wide eyes. 'Oh my, I've never seen anything so beautiful. See, Rose, you will look like a fairy princess in this gown.'

Rose peered in. With trembling fingers she raised the garment. A cloud of silver spangles fell about her arms; there was no other ornamentation. The material and cut of the gown made them redundant. Slowly she stood up and held it in front of her.

'It is a perfect size for you, my love, you will look like a diamond of the first water dressed in that.'

'But, Mama, it hardly seems fair that a lovely gown will change me into something I am not.'

'Fustian, my dear, and you know it. I

cannot imagine how you managed to catch the eye of Lord Bentley, but it is obvious from this gift that he thinks the world of you.'

Millie had been rummaging in the box. 'Look, there is a slipper bag, a silver domino and these must be the matching gloves.'

It seemed churlish to remain unmoved by all this magnificence.

'I must admit for a gentleman he has exquisite taste. How he knew what size to get I cannot think.'

She was trying on the slippers when Symonds appeared for a second time. 'Another delivery for Miss Bannerman. There's a letter with this one.'

Her sister was nearest and removed the second, smaller parcel from the bad-tempered footman. Quickly removing her slippers, which fitted perfectly of course, Rose scrambled up to sit on the sofa. Should she open the letter first, or the box? Two pairs of eyes were watching her every move and she wished she could take the missive somewhere private to read.

Biting her lip she broke the blob of wax and unfolded the crisp parchment. The black scrawl all but jumped off the page.

My dear,

I was remiss yesterday in not placing the ring upon your finger as I should have done. I hope you will forgive me. Enclosed also are the Bentley diamonds. I have spent another tedious hour recovering them from the bank.

Please wear them for me tonight.

Kindly inform Lady Bannerman I shall be calling for you in my carriage at nine o'clock.

I remain yours,

The black slash across the page must be his signature. Thank goodness this was something she could read aloud. When she had finished her mother shook her head in disbelief.

'Those stones are legendary, my love.

I do not believe they have been seen in public for many years. You are greatly honoured. Small wonder he wishes to escort his heirlooms himself. However, I cannot allow you to travel unescorted even though you are engaged. I shall write to Lord Bentley at once and tell him we shall meet at the ball.'

'Are you not going to show us, Rose?' Millie was eying the box with excitement.

'If I must.' Her mother's remark had stung; if even her own *parent* did not think her worthy, then how could she expect to engender respect, to earn affection, from him? The smaller box containing the betrothal ring could wait until last. She must undo the gold filigree fastening on the larger one first. This weighed heavy in her lap; it must contain several pieces.

She flipped the lid open and gasped. Inside was the most extravagant diamond necklace, ear bobs and a tiara. There were also two bracelets to match the rest. She was not surprised this had not been seen in public, there was a king's ransom here. Surely such items should only be worn on royal occasions?

'I shan't wear these tonight, Mama. I believe they should be kept for my wedding day, they are far too grand for a mere ball.'

'For once I agree with you, Rosamond. I think perhaps a compromise must be made. When you are dressed I shall come to your apartment and help you choose which pieces to wear. The betrothal ring — you have not looked at that. Whatever it's like, *that* must be prominently displayed.'

The ring was equally ostentatious. A huge square cut diamond surrounded by smaller stones. This would not suit her slim finger at all. 'Shall I try it on?' Her mother nodded vigorously. Rose slipped the ring over her knuckle and the weight of the stones immediately sent it sideways. 'I shall be terrified of losing this; the ring is far too big. I hope Lord Bentley understands.'

Preparing for the ball was a pleasure rather than a penance. She had decided to wear only the headpiece and ear bobs, any more would be too much. She stood in front of the full-length glass staring back at a stranger. 'Millie, I can't believe what a difference an expensive gown has made to my appearance. I feel like a princess from a fairy-tale.' Her lips curved as she thought of one particular heroine she would rather *not* be. 'As long as I am not Cinderella and my outfit turns to rags at midnight, I shall be happy.'

'You are even more beautiful tonight, Rose. Your partner will be the envy of every gentleman. No one will doubt he has made an excellent choice.'

'But I've only three items from the box he sent. And the ear bobs are not quite the same now I've removed half the stones.'

'Threading one of the clusters on that purple ribbon in order to wear it around your neck was a good idea for it completes your ensemble perfectly. The necklace is quite hideous. It's hardly surprising no one has seen a duchess wearing it in recent years.'

Mary swirled the silver domino around Rose's shoulders. 'There, miss, this is warmly lined so you will not be cold.'

Millie called out from her position by the window. 'Good gracious, Lord Bentley has come here after all. Do you think he didn't receive Mama's note?'

'What shall we do? I can hardly leave him sitting outside. I must go down and speak to him at least.'

On impulse Rose pulled on her gloves and tied a ribbon of her domino at her neck. She would not reveal how little of she had worn of the Duke's family heirlooms until they met later.

Symonds was waiting at the doorway and opened the door as she rushed up. 'I shall not be long, I must speak to the Duke.'

The carriage door swung open as she

left the house and he stepped out. 'Good evening, my dear, I'm glad to see you are a punctual young lady.'

'I am famous for my punctuality, your Grace. You have only to ask a member of my family and they will say the same.'

His rich, dark chuckle filled the night. 'Then should I be suspicious of your prompt arrival?'

She froze. He was far too astute to deceive. 'I'm afraid you are correct. There is something I must tell you . . . '

'Not out here on the pavement, sweetheart. I shall come in and you can tell me what has disturbed you.'

The ever vigilant Symonds threw open the front door with a flourish and bowed them into the vestibule.

Rose took a deep breath. 'I didn't wear all the jewels. They are too elaborate for someone my age.'

He chuckled. 'Is that a polite way of saying they are old-fashioned?'

She nodded. 'I think they are more suited to an older woman, and to a far grander occasion than tonight.'

'Sweetheart, this is my fault. To tell you the truth I did not bother to look at the contents of the box. If you say the jewellery is hideous then I shall take your word for it. I shall have it reset for you in a more modern design.'

'Oh, please do not. The jewellery has been as it is for so long it would be a pity to change it. The only item that needs resizing is the ring. I dare not wear it whilst it is so loose.'

'You must give it to me. Can you fetch it now?'

'No, it is safely locked with the other items in the safe in the study.'

'Then I shall collect it later. You will need to find me a ring of yours so that I can ensure this one is correctly sized. And now I must go, my dear. I only called in to give you this.' He dipped into his pocket and produced a slim, velvet box. 'I hope you will find this more to your taste. I shall be honoured if you wear it tonight for me.' He smiled and strode out into the night before she had time to thank him for his gift. She opened the box and gasped. Nestling on a silk bed was the prettiest silver locket she'd ever seen. Far better than the diamonds on the ribbon she was wearing.

She dashed upstairs and met Millie and Mama on their way down.

'La, child! Why dashing around like this — you will spoil your gown.'

Rose held out the box. 'I'm going to put this on. Lord Bentley came specially to give it to me.'

'How kind of him! He's obviously enamoured. Be quick, my dear, we mustn't keep the horses waiting.'

* * *

The drive was short but even so, Millie's chatter and her mother's constant reminders to behave made it seem interminable. The carriage stopped and two footmen opened the door and let down the steps. Burning flambeaux lit their way along the splendid red carpet. The house was abuzz with guests, for Lord Ponsonby was famous for his hospitality. Mama took the lead. Like a ship in full sail she entered the imposing vestibule, the monstrous feathers in her turban bobbing wildly in the flickering light.

'Millie, I feel quite different this evening. It must be this beautiful gown.'

'Not only that, dearest. The fact you are to marry the most eligible *parti* in England is making you more confident.' Millie clutched her arm. 'Over there, the Duke is waiting for you.'

There were dozens of others milling about in the spacious entrance hall, and a further queue of people slowly mounting the wide staircase which led to the ballroom on the first floor. However, she saw him immediately.

He was wearing a black evening cloak, but had adopted the new fashion of pantaloons and evening slippers. She didn't blame him, even the sturdiest of limbs did not look their best encased in silk stockings.

A flunky glided up beside him and he

deftly tossed his hat and gloves across, then unhooked his cloak and that joined the other items. He was dressed entirely in black, his waistcoat silver, his intricate cravat held in place by a single diamond pin. He looked magnificent. How could she have believed she was good enough for him? He could have chosen any girl but her behaviour had forced him to take her. It would not do. Somehow she would extricate them both from this tangle, find a way to release him and leave him free to find himself a suitable bride. But not tonight — she would have just this one evening to enjoy being the future bride of a Duke.

'I must speak to him. Tell Mama I have gone to the retiring room.'

'Be quick, Rose. She is talking to a friend and will not notice you have gone for a few minutes at least.'

She couldn't approach him in full view of the arriving guests. Where could she go? He was already moving purposefully in her direction so could follow her. There was a quiet alcove on the far side of the vestibule. They would still be visible, but not so prominent as before. And suddenly she realised that with all the talk about the diamonds outside her house she had quite forgotten to thank him for her beautiful gown . . .

★ ★ ★

Perry had never seen anything so lovely as the girl standing wide-eyed in front of him. A wave of something he did not recognize rushed through him. Since the debacle yesterday he had resigned himself to the inevitable, but now everything had changed.

'I cannot wait to see you in your finery. I hope you have noticed my attire is worn to complement *your* ensemble.'

'This is my first official ball, sir. Apart from the other night I have not attended any similar functions.'

His hand touched hers briefly. 'I am

delighted to hear you say so; with luck everyone will forget that first appearance.'

She untied the ribbon of her cloak and removed it. He caught his breath.

'You are *ravisante*. That gown is perfect. You must never wear anything but silver in future. I shall be the envy of every gentleman tonight.'

'I should have thanked you straightaway, your Grace. I feel like a princess. I cannot think how you could have arranged such a thing so quickly.'

'My sister knew exactly what to do. My only worry was the slippers might be uncomfortable.' Her smile transformed her face. Why did she not do so more often?

'They are perfect. Tonight I shall pretend I am someone important, for dressed like this I shall not be looked down on.'

He took her hands and drew her close to him. 'No one will ever insult you again, my love. You're under my protection. As my future wife they will have to answer to me.'

He looked so fierce on her behalf she could not help herself. She touched his hand. 'You are a kind man. I believe I could come to like you when you are not scowling and taking me to task.'

His look of stupefaction was worth the breach of protocol. Gathering up the skirt of her silver dress she spun and hurried back to join her sister and mother.

'Rosamond, what were you thinking of? Has there not already been enough talk about your fast behaviour?'

'I was just thanking him for his gifts. I believe as his betrothed it is for him to say if my behaviour is displeasing.' Taking her sister's arm she fled to the relative safety of one of the ladies' retiring rooms.

'Millie, I don't know what gets into me when I am with him. I behave quite outrageously. He was so pleased with me and now I will have disgusted him again.'

'He was smiling in a most particular way, Rose. If he was cross he has a remarkable way of showing it.'

'Am I perfect in every detail, Millie? No smuts on my nose?'

'You are. You look beautiful. I'm so excited Sir Richard is to join us as well. I should think the Duke will wish to introduce you to his family tonight.' She twirled and the golden curls flew out around her.

'Enough, Millie, you will disarrange your hair.'

'Imagine! Our party will be escorted by two of the most eligible gentleman in Town.'

'I know; we must be on our best behaviour.'

When they returned to the vestibule the area was more crowded. She had no difficulty locating her partner for he stood a head above everyone else. His eyes met hers and he surged towards her. Where other lesser mortals might have had to ask guests to excuse him, he knew they would step aside to let him through. It must be a strange sensation being so important. He nodded to her sister but drew her apart.

'At last! Only by my fiercest expression have I been able to forestall a plethora of hopeful young ladies. Word of our betrothal has obviously not filtered through society as yet. We must endeavour to mention it to everyone we meet. Lady Bannerman, Miss Amelia, shall we go?'

He tucked her arm securely through his and guided her to the staircase. At his side it did not seem so daunting being the centre of attention. He smiled down at her and she responded.

'Come, I wish to introduce you to my sister and my youngest niece. It is her first season also.'

'I take it there's a considerable age difference between you and your sister?'

'Sixteen years. I have three older sisters. My parents had despaired of producing a son and then I arrived most unexpectedly.' His expression was sombre.

'Unfortunately, having a child so late in life proved disastrous to my mother's health. She died when I was still in leading strings. My father was heart-broken.'

'I am sorry for your loss. It must have been difficult growing up without your mother.'

He raised an eyebrow. 'I was the most spoilt child in the kingdom. Everyone from my papa to the loneliest minion was there to serve me. I believe this is why I have — as you have frequently told me — such a high opinion of myself. I was educated to think I was a superior being.'

The Duke was such fun when in this teasing mood.

'Am I to apologise for speaking the truth?'

His mouth curved in a tender smile. 'Do you know, sweetheart, you are the first person to have had the temerity to say so. I think your candour attracted me.' For no apparent reason his smile vanished and the muscles bunched under her hand. He was once again a formidable aristocrat.

7

Perry cursed his inadvertent comment. The last thing he wanted to do was to give her the impression he had anything other than the mildest interest in her as a woman. She was scarcely out of the schoolroom, far too young to be frightened by such things. Had he not already overstepped the mark by kissing her? Time enough, when they had been married a while, to gently introduce her to the pleasures of the marriage bed. Although worldly in some ways, in this matter she was very much an innocent. He must treat her as he would his niece and not alarm her in any way.

He glanced down; she was walking proudly at his side, every inch a duchess in waiting. She had spent her life being compared unfavourably to her sister; from now on things would be different. She would be treated with respect, admired and feted by all who met her. Why, within a few weeks she could be exactly the bride he had always wanted, beautiful, intelligent and obedient to his wishes. He would not complicate matters by showing her unwanted affection. She had made it abundantly clear that, given a choice, she would not marry him at all.

In her silver-heeled slippers and tiara she was almost as tall as him. It made a pleasant change to escort a young lady who did not make him feel like a clumsy giant. His lips curved when he remembered the touch given so guilelessly; could it be that her opinion on this union were also undergoing a *volte face?*

★ ★ ★

The silence had gone on for too long, she could not bear it. 'Lord Bentley, are you to dance tonight? What should I do if another gentleman wishes to escort me?'

His head shot round. His eyes were

121

fierce. 'I would prefer you to dance only with me, my dear, but unfortunately it would not be fair to ask you to refuse other partners.'

Good heavens — if she did not know better she might think his reaction that of jealousy. She smiled sweetly, ignoring his frown. 'And which dances, your Grace, shall we perform?' She was trying not to show her amusement. An imp of mischief prompted her to tease him further. 'Indeed, sir, might we not waltz without permission? After all, you are such an illustrious personage no one could possibly object.'

His laughter turned several heads. 'You're a baggage, my love. It would serve you right if I insisted on dancing every single dance with you and cause further scandal.'

'It would be more a punishment for you, I am a poor partner. I always trip over something and usually it's my own feet.'

'With me it shall be different. I am, of course, the most able dancer here tonight.' This was said with a commendably straight face. Rose was seeing a different side to him tonight. Perhaps he was not so high in the instep if he could poke fun at himself like this.

They reached the head of the line and curtsied and bowed their way along it. Once released, he took her hand again and led her through the crowds. Her mother and sister trailed along behind. He stopped at the edge of the ballroom where the musicians in the gallery were tuning up.

'Remember, sweetheart, the waltz is mine.'

'I do not know half of the dances. We shall both look ridiculous if I join a set for one of those.'

His fingertips lightly brushed her cheek. 'I only intend to dance when it is a waltz.'

'With you glowering at my side I don't think anyone else would dare to approach.'

He chuckled. 'I shall not be with you every moment. I'm certain you will be surrounded by young gallants eager to escort you on the dance floor. Now, if you will forgive me, there are gentlemen I have to speak to.'

The first waltz was not for an hour at least. She had no wish to dance with anyone else but if she didn't she would be obliged to sit like a wallflower.

Her mother bustled up. 'Rosamund, Amelia, come with me. We must secure a place on the edge of the ballroom. With such a press here tonight there are not likely to be empty seats for long.'

'Mama, I do not wish to dance with anyone apart from the Duke. May I have your permission to find somewhere quiet to wait?'

'No, my dear, you must stay with me. Goodness knows what mischief you will get up to on your own.'

Sir Richard arrived at their side. 'Good evening, Lady Bannerman. Allow me to escort you to a comfortable corner.'

'Thank you, Sir Richard, most kind of you.'

Rose stepped aside, allowing her sister

to walk next to him. As they were moving through the crush an elegant lady accosted her.

'Miss Bannerman, my brother was to have introduced us. I am Lady Laura Foster, and this is my daughter, Charlotte.'

Millie, Mama and Sir Richard had forged on, not realising Rose had been obliged to stop. She curtsied and smiled at her future sister-in-law. 'My lady, I must thank you for obtaining this beautiful gown at such short notice.'

'I was pleased to be of assistance, my dear. To see my brother thinking of someone else's comfort for a change made me realize, however unfortunate the beginning of this betrothal, that you are obviously the right bride for him.'

Rose curtsied. 'I sincerely hope you are right, my lady.' She soon discovered her sister and mama happily ensconced in a small alcove away from the press of people. Sir Richard was sitting with them and jumped to his feet as she arrived.

'Miss Rosamund, please take my seat. If it should be left empty for a moment some other wretch will steal it away.'

'Then I shall be seated immediately. I am delighted to meet you again, Sir Richard. Millie has already told me so much about you.'

'I have, we were just discussing how odd it is that both of us should have been rescued from that oak tree by the very men we are now . . . ' Millie flushed scarlet.

Sir Richard instantly dropped to one knee attracting a deal of unwanted attention by his dramatic gesture. This was neither the place nor the time to make a declaration, but there was no stopping him. He was as impulsive as her sister.

'Amelia, my love, will you do me the inestimable honour of becoming my wife?'

Her sister clapped her hands. 'I will, you know I will.'

'Sir Richard, you are making a cake

of yourself. Get up, please.' Rose laughed.

Quite unrepentant he grinned and bounced upright. 'There, now you are both engaged to be married to the men who saved you from the oak tree all those years ago.' He bowed in the direction of Mama. 'Lady Bannerman, I apologise if I have embarrassed you. I know I should have spoken to you first, but I could not have my darling think I didn't love her enough to speak in public.'

Her mother beamed at her future son-in-law. 'It would have been better to have done things in the more normal way; however I am delighted to welcome you to the family. My dear husband will not believe it when he returns in a week or two. Both my daughters engaged, and to such splendid gentlemen.'

Word of this would already be flying around the ballroom and it would not be long before it reached the ears of the Duke. She sincerely hope that he would be as amused as she was by the incident.

She kissed her sister. 'I'm happy for you. I'm glad you have found the man of *your* dreams.' Whilst her mother was occupied with Sir Richard and Millie she took the opportunity to slip away. Several hopeful gentlemen had been drifting in her direction obviously intending to ask her to stand up with them. She had no intention of remaining in the ballroom. Surely there must be somewhere she could sit and compose herself in this vast establishment? She would seek out the library or some other quiet place.

The wide corridor was empty. The noise from upstairs created a background hum. She heard the orchestra begin to play. She paused, listening. This was a set dance — there would be two parts to it.

Her sister's sudden engagement was an added problem. Mama had made it very plain that one of them must marry money in order to save the family. Sir

Richard was not wealthy which meant the responsibility was on her shoulders. Breaking off her engagement was no longer an option.

The third door she opened was a small drawing-room. A fire burned brightly in the grate giving sufficient light to see the room was empty. She ignited a candle from the flames. Selecting a small upholstered chair, she smoothed her gown and sat down carefully. The music filtered down from the ballroom above. It should be simple enough to work out when she should return.

★　★　★

Perry was arranging to view a team of thoroughbreds owned by a crony of his. He didn't need any more horses, but this opportunity was too good to miss. He had wanted to purchase this particular set of chestnuts since he saw them last spring. He was not impressed on being interrupted by an acquaintance he always did his best to avoid.

'My word, Bentley, have you heard the latest? Devonshire has just made Miss Amelia Bannerman on offer in full view of dozens of people. An eccentric family, wouldn't you say?'

What next? Richard had always been impulsive. No doubt he considered himself head over ears in love and had been chivvied into declaring himself. He had better go and tell Rose before she heard it from someone else.

He could see his niece dancing and Miss Amelia, but there was no sign of Rose. She must be sitting with her mother somewhere. He picked out Lady Bannerman and scanned the row of gilt chairs. Rose was nowhere to be seen. He looked more closely at the couples on the floor; she was not dancing either.

It should be easy enough to find her even in this throng. As he was threading his way across an ante-room he came face-to-face with Richard and his future bride. 'Congratulations, Richard. I hope you will not want a double wedding?'

Immediately Miss Amelia nodded. 'What a wonderful idea, your Grace. After all, Rose and I are twins and you and Sir Richard good friends.'

God forbid! He schooled his features before answering. 'I am looking for your sister, is she with Lady Bannerman?'

'No, she left some time ago.'

Keeping his disquiet to himself, he smiled and excused himself. It took him a further quarter of an hour to be certain Rose was not upstairs. This meant she must be in one of the ladies' retiring rooms.

He waylaid a maid and sent her to enquire. A few minutes later the girl returned. She curtsied nervously. 'Your Grace, Miss Bannerman has not been in any of the rooms set aside. I have no idea where she might be.'

Waving the woman away, he frowned. Where would a girl go in a house she did not know? There were several doors further up the corridor. He would try those before setting up a search party. He knocked, received no answer and opened the door. The room was in darkness; there was no one inside here.

When he opened the second one there was light inside. Slowly he stepped in. His breath caught in his throat; he had never seen anything so lovely. Curled up on a fireside chair was the girl he sought. She was fast asleep with her glorious dress spread out around her and her face resting on one hand. How could he have ever thought her plain? She was the most beautiful girl in the world and she had agreed to marry *him*. Somehow he must convince her she was not making a sacrifice but stepping into a future full of wonderful possibilities.

Should he wake her or leave her to sleep? Undecided, he stepped closer and stubbed his toe on the chair leg that had been hidden by her skirts. He could not hold back his curse. His feet were as unprotected as a girl's in these wretched slippers.

★ ★ ★

Rose heard him swear and sat up her eyes wide with apprehension. She pressed herself against the chair back waiting for him to roar at her. He was quite terrifying when he was in a rage. She managed to stutter a few words. 'Please, do not be angry, I did not mean to fall asleep. Have I missed our first waltz?'

He dropped into a chair opposite, his expression tender and no sign of irritation at all. 'I beg your pardon for using such language in your presence, sweetheart. I crushed my toe. I fear I might be unable to dance at all.'

'I do hope you have not broken it. There is nothing worse than the pain of a damaged toe. How did you find me?' Her brow furrowed. 'More to the point, sir, why are you here at all?'

'I heard about your sister's engagement and came to warn you. When I discovered you were not upstairs I became concerned you might be unwell. I thought it sensible to explore these chambers before involving anyone else in my search.'

She was embarrassed to be found sleeping like a child by her future husband. She was a woman grown and for some reason this was a point she wished to make very clear between them. Dropping her feet to the floor she stood. There was no need to rearrange her gown as it flowed around her naturally.

She waited. He unfolded from the chair. That peculiar darkness was in his eyes again. She held out her hand. He hesitated then moved fast. His arms encircled her waist and she was lifted from her feet and crushed against his chest with such passion her head spun. Her head tilted of its own volition and his mouth closed over hers. His lips were hard, demanding something she did not know how to give him.

Then they softened, left her bruised mouth and began a magic trail from her jaw line to her shoulder. She relaxed into his embrace and strange warmth engulfed her. With what sounded more like a groan than speech he kissed her lips a second time and released her. For a second she thought her knees would give way and then she recovered her composure. He had, like the other time, turned his back on her.

'Have I upset you? Should I not have been so forward?'

'Yet again I have behaved disgracefully.' He swung back. His face was hard to see at the far side of the room. 'I shall wait for you in the vestibule.'

Fortunately there was a small glass on the wall above a side table. From the light of the single candlestick she restored her appearance. The lovely diamond tiara had slipped sideways at a rakish angle and the shoulder of her gown was similarly disarranged.

She was still unsure if what had taken place between them was a good thing or a bad. She had only wanted to demonstrate she was an adult. He had misinterpreted her gesture as an invitation to . . . to take liberties. One thing she was certain, such behaviour was only permissible between couples who were betrothed. Whatever her wishes she feared she was irretrievably entangled. She must marry a man she wasn't sure she liked and who quite possibly despised her.

It would not do to be tardy for he was not a patient man. Her heart skipped a beat when she saw him striding up and down the all but empty vestibule. The more she saw of him the more she was forced to admit he was the most attractive man she had ever set eyes on.

'Come, my love, we shall dance. I assume you have learned the steps of the waltz?'

'I have, and sometimes I even perform them correctly.'

His smile was beguiling. 'I have an ingenious solution. Why don't you stand on my toes. Nobody would know as the length of your skirts will disguise this. That way you can be sure of making no mistakes.'

Her gurgle of laughter attracted attention. 'I shall do no such thing. You assured me you are the best dancer in Town so I shall rely on your expertise to guide me.'

Couples were already drifting onto the polished floor and an air of expectancy hung over the room. She could sense the beady eyes of the matrons seated around the floor boring into her back. She was unmoved. The Duke was there to protect her good name now. He was a law unto himself. He did as he pleased knowing Society would forgive him. Hopefully, in future, her transgressions would also be over-looked.

The violins soared, filling the space with the beautiful notes of a waltz. She placed one hand on his shoulder, the other in his. The heat from his hand scorched through the thin material of her gown. She was being branded by his imprint.

Surefooted he guided her around the floor. For the first time the steps made sense. She glided beside him as if she had been performing this dance every day of her life. Slowly he tightened his hold until they were dancing far closer than was considered proper. She became part of him.

'This is the most amazing sensation, your Grace. I feel as if I am floating on air.'

His eyes burned into hers. 'Tonight you're my silver angel. Small wonder you are flying.'

They twirled around the floor. She was oblivious to everything but the music and the man holding her so possessively to his heart. She felt him stiffen and looked up anxiously. His lopsided grin made her stomach somersault.

'I hate to tell you this, darling girl, but we have the floor to ourselves. No, do not hesitate, we are invincible tonight.'

8

Somehow Rose managed to complete the dance without showing her disquiet. He seemed unperturbed by being the centre of attention. He continued to lead the way around the floor as if he frequently danced in public.

Eventually the music died. She wanted to run away, but he held her steady. A spontaneous burst of applause echoed around the ballroom and his fingers dug into her waist. 'Smile, my dear. Take it in your stride.'

Held close to him as she was, she could do nothing else. She smiled as instructed, but directed it at him. For a delicious moment she thought he would kiss her in front of the assembled crowd. Then he recovered and swept her across the floor. He nodded graciously at all who congratulated them on their solo performance, but did not pause until they were safely away from the crush.

'We shall be safe here for supper is not to be served until after the next dance. Don't look so stricken, little one, tonight you have conquered society.'

The mention of food made her stomach gurgle. She had been too nervous to eat. Nothing had passed her lips since first thing this morning. 'I am not upset, your Grace . . .'

'Enough. I am heartily sick of hearing you calling me 'your Grace'.'

'I call you 'Lord Bentley 'as well, and I believe that sometimes I say 'sir'. I don't lard my conversation with unnecessary endearments. If you agree to use my given name, without embellishment, then I shall agree to address you however you wish.'

'Then in future you may use my given name. I take it you do know what it is.'

'Peregrine, but I believe your intimates are allowed to call you Perry.'

His look sent warning signals flashing

around her already overheated body. 'I give you permission to call me Perry. Now, from the ominous rumblings I've been hearing from the direction of your middle, I take it you are hungry.'

'I am ravenous. I was trying to tell you your . . . Perry. That is why I look pained, no other reason I do assure you.' She viewed the loaded buffet table eagerly. 'Do you think Lady Ponsonby would object if we help ourselves?'

'By the time we have what we want the doors will be open and everyone else will have flooded in.' He nodded at the row of wigged footmen standing rigid against the far wall. He raised a hand in the direction of the table and instantly two servants hurried forward to attend to his needs.

'Is there anything you particularly want? I can see lobster patties, salmon in aspic, every possible variety of cold meat and all the condiments to go with them.'

'I love lobster patties, and salmon . . .' She sighed. 'In fact I like everything you've mentioned. Perhaps we could taste everything?'

The hovering footmen rushed to fill their plates. Perry took her to a small table tucked discreetly behind a pillar. There were already name cards on this. He removed them and handed them to a waiting servant. 'Deal with these. We are sitting here.'

During the ten minutes they were obliged to wait for their food he was at his most charming. Was he also changing his opinion of her, as she was of him? From behind the enormous flower arrangement a footman appeared.

'Good grief! A second table? Why do we need this?' She was to discover the answer as a further four servants appeared, each carrying plates piled high with food. Rose was about to point out they did not want so much when Perry shook his head.

She watched in awe as five dishes of savouries were arranged on the table at which they sat. The other three were of sweet things and they were placed on the spare one. Next empty plates were placed in front of each of them and further crockery for the desserts. A jug of lemonade and a bottle of claret were somehow squeezed onto the cloth.

Perry leaned back in his chair and spoke quietly to the senior man. The footman nodded and smiled happily before leading his troop back to face the army of hungry guests about to descend.

'I have never seen so much food. I did not know I would be taken literally.'

'Nothing will go to waste. You can be assured the footmen who fetched the food for us will enjoy a tasty supper when they finish tonight.'

Afterwards Rose could not recall what they spoke about. The food was delicious and she ate far more than was good for her. Eventually replete, she wiped her mouth on her napkin and smiled at him. 'Even though we have both dined well, we have barely made inroads on what was given to us.'

Perry came round to pull back her

chair. He nodded at one of the footmen and they picked up the tables and vanished through a side door with them. The supper room was full, making it impossible to converse without raising one's voice over the noise of chatter and cutlery.

'The ballroom will be quiet. Shall we stroll around there or would you rather sit?'

'Walk, if you please, I am far too full to remain stationary. Look, there is Mama, she is beckoning me. Pray excuse me, I must go and speak to her as she will be wondering where I have been all this while. I suppose I should not have come into supper with you unchaperoned.'

He raised an eyebrow. 'You are my future wife, I'm sure our breach of protocol will be forgiven. I shall leave you with your mother. I must try and find my friend and resume my attempts to persuade him to sell me his chestnuts. He is proving remarkably stubborn on this matter.'

'Shall you be long?'

He grinned down at her and she felt something strange flicker through her. 'I sincerely hope not, sweetheart. I shall prevail in the end. Run along, my dear, and I shall come and find you after the supper interval.'

A faint unease replaced the excitement. She was in a fair way to falling back in love with him but his tendency to treat her like a silly schoolgirl was beginning to be irksome. She would give the matter some thought. Somehow she must prove to him she was an adult. She wished to be treated with respect and not talked down to or patronised in any way.

Her mother greeted her with effusion. 'My dear girl, you are the talk of the evening. My word, I had no idea you were such a proficient dancer. Monsieur Duclos, the Frenchman I engaged to tutor you and your sister, was forever complaining of your clumsiness.' Her mother stared eagerly at the sumptuous buffet. 'We must lay claim to a table before they are all gone.'

Immediately Richard bowed. 'Allow me, my lady. Wait there and I will call you over when I have found something suitable.'

Millie took her hands and squeezed them. 'Rose, don't you dare tell me you are the plain sister ever again. There is something about Lord Bentley that brings out the sparkle in your eyes.' She turned to gaze adoringly at her own partner directing a harassed footman. 'Richard and I have been given permission to waltz — shall you and Lord Bentley be joining us after supper for a second turn about the floor?'

'Absolutely not. I have made a sufficient exhibition of myself for one evening. When he returns we are to stroll around the ballroom. I have already eaten my supper; I'm far too full to sit down with any degree of comfort.'

'Come along, girls, Sir Richard is beckoning.'

'Mama, Lord Bentley and I have

already eaten. Am I permitted to walk around the ballroom until you have finished?'

'Yes, my dear, that will be quite acceptable. Ensure that you remain in full view at all times.'

Rose was aware she was attracting an undue amount of attention, especially from the young unattached gentlemen. She had no wish to receive their fulsome compliments, and was quite certain Lord Bentley . . . no, she must think of him as Perry from now on . . . would not take kindly to it either. She glanced about in desperation and espied her future niece, Charlotte. She would join her.

'Miss Foster, forgive me, I am waiting for Lord Bentley but he seems to be delayed. Would you mind very much if I walked with you until he returns?'

'Please do. My uncle wishes us to be friends. I cannot think how you have persuaded him to give up his freedom. Why, only the other day he was assuring my mama that he had no intention of marrying anyone.' The girl flushed scarlet and clapped her gloved hands to her mouth as if trying to push the words back in.

Rose forced herself to smile and repeated the story they had concocted. 'We have known each other more than five years. He saved me from a nasty accident and I have loved him ever since. However, I was surprised to discover he reciprocated my feelings.'

Lady Laura Foster arrived at their side. 'There you are. I have been looking for you this age, my dear. We must go into supper or we shall be still at the table when the dancing resumes.' She beamed at Rose. 'My brother is in the card room, Miss Bannerman. He looks as if he will be occupied for some time. I think it would be unwise of you to wait here alone, my dear. Would you like to come with us? You could sit and drink lemonade whilst we eat.'

'No, thank you, my lady. If Lord Bentley is playing cards then I shall retire to a small withdrawing-room I discovered earlier. No doubt he will find me when he is done.'

Downstairs was pleasantly quiet and far cooler than the ballroom or the dining room. A helpful footman came over to offer his assistance. 'Is it possible for me to sit in the library?'

'Follow me, Miss Bannerman. I'm sure the master will have no objection to you waiting there for Lord Bentley.'

How did this lowly minion know her identity and to whom she was betrothed? Quite alarming to think these things were already common knowledge below stairs. Once she was married to the Duke she would have no privacy at all, for her every move would be scrutinised and reported on. She would not be allowed to gallivant around the countryside in her oldest clothes or spend happy hours in the stables with her beloved horses. Perry had high standards and she would be expected to conform.

A shiver of apprehension trickled down her spine. She had not yet reached her eighteenth name day — she wasn't ready to be curtailed in this way. The liveried servant bowed and politely pushed open one of a pair of imposing double doors.

'Thank you. Could you please inform Lord Bentley of my whereabouts? He is playing cards upstairs somewhere.'

The library was pleasantly warm. She would not be cold even in her diaphanous ball gown. She wandered across to the nearest book lined wall and selected a leather bound volume at random. Blowing the dust from its spine, she carried it to the nearest armchair. Earlier in the evening she had fallen asleep and her gown had not suffered. If she was careful she could curl up for an hour or so to read and still return to the ball with it relatively uncreased.

Unfortunately the book she chose was a tiresome volume of sermons. With a sigh she scrambled up quite forgetting she had spread her gown around her feet. There was an ominous ripping as her heeled slipper tore through the spangles. Horrified she dropped the book. The heavy tome landed on the flimsy material and compounded the damage.

Her beautiful gown was ruined and so was her evening. She must return home at once. Her dress was hanging in tatters about her ankles. She recalled her earlier mention of not wishing to be like Cinderella. This catastrophe placed her in a similar situation. She looked around and saw the bell strap by the over mantel and quickly pulled it.

A parlour maid appeared through a door hidden between the shelves, almost giving her an apoplexy. 'I have, as you can see, quite spoiled my ball gown. It is beyond repair. I wish to have my carriage brought round immediately. There's no need to send messages to my family right away. I would be grateful if you would inform them *after* I have left.'

The girl curtsied. 'I shall fetch your cloak immediately, Miss Bannerman. I shall send word for your carriage to be brought round and come and fetch you when it's outside.'

Scarcely twenty minutes later the girl returned with the silver domino over her arm. Rose swirled it around her shoulders. The voluminous folds hid the damage perfectly. She followed the maid through the deserted passage-ways, across the vast vestibule, and out to the waiting vehicle. She scrambled in and a footman put away the steps. The coachman snapped his whip and the carriage trundled homewards.

The interior was freezing after the warmth of the house. She huddled in the corner unable to prevent tears from spilling down her cheeks. Why was she so clumsy? Millie would never have put her foot through *her* ball gown in this stupid fashion. Wearing this lovely garment had merely disguised her true nature. She was not meant to be a duchess. She was a simple country girl and could never be happy anywhere else.

Only as the carriage rocked and

bumped its way towards Grosvenor Square did she remember she had not asked the servant to take a message to Perry. He would discover she had gone when he went to the library to look for her. This entire situation was untenable. He must no longer be Perry in her thoughts . . . she would break off the engagement. She would come up with a scheme to persuade him that temporary public opprobrium was far better than a lifetime tied to a totally unsuitable wife.

* * *

Perry had reluctantly agreed to play a hand of cards. He did not wish to be away from Rose too long. She was the belle of the ball and a young buck might attempt to cut him out. He was nine years her senior and it was possible she could prefer someone nearer her own age.

He frowned, and then relaxed. She would be safe enough with her mother and sister for the moment, so it would do no harm to butter up Sir John. He was more likely to agree to sell his chestnuts if he did so. His lips curved — she had said so herself — he was the most eligible bachelor in the country. No young lady — not even one as unconventional as Rose — would wish to pass up the chance of becoming a duchess.

A hovering footman obviously had a message of some sort. Perry crooked a finger and the man slid over. Rose was safely in the library. Excellent! He could enjoy a hand or two before going down to retrieve her.

Less than an hour later he pushed open the door to find the room empty. Puzzled he called her name, but got no response. Where the devil was she? He seemed to have spent the majority of the evening searching for her. She must have become bored with waiting and returned to the ballroom. The second waltz was about to be performed and he had every intention of leading her out.

He strode back upstairs. He scanned the crowds for her but she was nowhere to be seen. Then he saw Lady Bannerman; he would ask this redoubtable lady what had happened to her daughter. He stopped in front of her, and bowed briefly. 'My lady, I am in search of Miss Bannerman. We are supposed to perform the next dance and I cannot find her anywhere.'

'My goodness! Where has the wretched girl got to? I was told she was waiting for you in the library. If she is not there I have no notion where she might be.' She surged to her feet opening and shutting her fan noisily. 'Perhaps Amelia will know where her sister is. Sir Richard has just this moment led her to the dance floor. Botheration! The music has started, now I must wait until the waltz has finished. It would not do to interrupt.'

The garrulous lady paused to draw breath and he quickly filled the brief gap.

'Lady Bannerman, I'm sure there is

nothing untoward in Miss Bannerman's temporary disappearance. I shall make further enquiries from the staff and get back to you as soon as I may.'

After a further frustrating period of time he eventually discovered a member of Ponsonby's staff who actually knew what had happened. By this time he was more than a little irritated. He was not accustomed to wasting his time. Why on earth had Rose not sent a message to him? Such thoughtlessness did not seem in character. He sent the footman to Lady Bannerman with the information that her daughter had returned to Grosvenor Square as her dress had been irreparably torn.

It had been a decidedly odd evening. When he had seen Rose asleep in the chair he had felt a faint stirring in the region of his heart. However, this flickering had subsided to be replaced by irritation. Sir John was still refusing to relinquish his chestnuts which added to his annoyance. Tomorrow he would make it abundantly clear that he did not take kindly to being treated with such incivility by his future bride.

He snapped his fingers and sent a minion running round to fetch his own carriage. The evening had not ended well for either of them. Rose must have been devastated at having to leave early in such an ignominious way. His ill-humour vanished. He was a selfish brute thinking only of his own inconvenience when she must have been in shreds. This was why she had not sent a message. She had been too distressed to think clearly. In the morning he would send round the *modiste* Laura had recommended and have all three ladies replenish their wardrobe at his expense. Smiling a little he ducked into his carriage. He settled in the corner, stretched out his legs and closed his eyes. One thing was certain; life would never be dull being involved with the Bannerman family.

9

Rose woke to the sound of rattling curtains and a delicious aroma of chocolate. She rubbed her eyes and pushed herself up on her elbows. Millie was still curled on the far side of the huge bed fast asleep. Rose had no idea when her sister had eventually returned.

She had intended to rise early and take Orion into the park for a gallop, but it was far too late to do that now. The smiling chambermaid bobbed and carefully set down a tray.

'Thank you, Elsie, leave it there. I shall pour it myself in a while. Could you send Mary in to me?'

Carefully pulling back the coverlet she slipped out, not wishing to wake her sister. The dressing room door swung open and her abigail appeared.

'Whatever happened to your lovely

gown, Miss Rose? I don't reckon it can be repaired.'

A sleepy voice called out from the bed. 'Yes, dearest, tell me at once how you came to ruin your dress.'

'I put my foot through the skirt and then dropped a book onto the tear. If I had remained in the ballroom, as Mama suggested, the disaster would have been averted.' She turned to Mary waiting politely in the background. 'I shall not be riding this morning so I shall wear the new velvet gown; the one without the frills and furbelows.'

'I'm quite ravenous, please pour me some chocolate and butter me two rolls, Rose. I'm feeling far too lazy to get out and do so myself.'

Rose completed this task willingly and pulled over a footstool to lean against the bed whilst she drank. She had no appetite this morning. She was torn by the necessity of breaking her engagement in order to save Lord Bentley from making a disastrous marriage and her wish to save the family's finances. Also

Millie's happiness was paramount; her betrothal could not continue if Rose's was broken. She sighed heavily and a mop of golden curls appeared over the side of the bed.

'What's wrong, Rose? You sound so sad and you should be bursting with joy after becoming the talk of the ball last night.'

'What happened made me understand I am not cut out to be a duchess. I am clumsy and outspoken, I do not care much for etiquette and the rules that govern society. Lord Bentley would never have considered me if I had not forced him to make me an offer.'

'But things are quite different now . . . I told you, everyone is talking about how Lord Bentley has finally fallen in love. You are the envy of every young lady in London.'

Chocolate slopped in her lap at her sister's unexpected words and she viewed the spreading stain with resignation. 'Look what I have done.' She scrambled to her feet putting down the half empty bowl. 'You are talking fustian, Millie, people see what they expect to see. Lord Bentley and I were playing our parts to perfection. He does not love me and I do not love him.'

'Fiddlesticks to that! He is besotted with you, and I'm certain you recipro-cate his feelings in full measure. Two people could not dance the way you did last night if they were not madly in love.'

'I refuse to discuss it further. I have made up my mind ... ' Her voice trailed away at the sound of running footsteps approaching the bed chamber. The door burst open and their mother rushed in clutching a letter to her heaving bosom.

'Disaster! Ruination! Where is your papa when he is wanted? We are undone, quite bankrupt. I have here a letter from the lawyers saying the mortgage has been called in. What shall I do? Rose, tell me how to proceed. We shall be evicted from our home. At any moment the bailiffs shall come and all our neighbours shall know what dire straits we are in.'

'Please let me read the letter, Mama, matters might not be as bad as you imagine.' Rose removed the paper from unresisting fingers and quickly scanned the contents. Indeed the news was quite as bad, if not worse, than Mama had intimated. Word had reached the bank that Papa's investments had turned to dust and the bank was intending to foreclose. She swallowed, her knuckles white. 'It will not come to that. I shall ask Lord Bentley to deal with the matter, I'm certain he would not wish his future family to become the subject of unpleasant gossip.'

Millie tumbled out of bed and rushed to offer comfort. 'Hush, Mama, do not take on so. Rose is quite right; Lord Bentley will deal with this. Papa can make things right when he returns.'

'But your dear father's ships were lost. That's why he went to India with David to try and discover where they went. They might well return no better off than when they left. I thank the good Lord for sending Lord Bentley to us, Rose. I shall send at once for him and beg him to intervene.'

The thought of what this letter might contain made Rose shudder. 'Mama, I think it might be better if I apply to him myself. I shall write at once and explain the situation.'

Millie gently took their mother's arm. 'Come, I shall take you back to your apartment, Mama. You are distressed. Why don't you lie down for a while and leave Rose to sort things out?'

This changed everything. She must put aside her doubts and resign herself to marrying the Duke. As soon as her sister and mother departed she hurriedly dressed. She could not contemplate writing what was tantamount to a begging letter unless she was properly attired.

Seated at her small bureau she sharpened her pen, uncorked the ink pot, spread out a sheet of fresh paper and was ready to write. However she was at a loss to know what to put; she was not fond of writing letters at the best of times. Every time she picked up the pen an image of the Duke's face filled her head. She could see, as if he was standing beside her, how his eyes would narrow and his lips thin when he read her missive. He would be outraged at her presumption, disgusted she was already dipping into his pockets in this way.

Black blots marred the pristine page; she would have to start again. Hopefully she would not spoil the second piece as this was the last sheet she had. There was no point in procrastinating. She must state her case and leave him to decide whether he wished to offer financial assistance.

Dear Lord Bentley
My family is facing financial ruin. My mother expects the bailiffs to arrive at any moment otherwise I would not be writing to you in this way.
You told me you were happy to

spend your wealth on my family, and I am hoping you are prepared to help us out of this difficulty. When my father and brother return they will, of course, reimburse you.

Yours very sincerely
Rose
PS: I do apologise for abandoning you last night, but I put my foot through my gown and had to return home immediately.

She sanded and folded the paper before she could change her mind. A blob of sealing wax completed the task. She scribbled his name and direction on the front. She rang the bell. 'Mary, please take this downstairs and ask for it to be delivered immediately.'

Millie returned as Rose was preparing to go. 'Mama is lying down, Cook has sent up a soothing tisane. She is most unwell. I do wish Papa and David were here. I don't like the house in an uproar like this.'

'Don't fret, dearest one, everything

will work out. Now, let me help you dress. Is Sir Richard to call round this morning?'

'Yes, I shall wear the yellow silk with the gold flounces.' Her sister noticed the disarray on the bureau. 'Have you written the letter to Lord Bentley already?'

'Indeed, there was not a moment to lose. We must be downstairs ready to receive our visitors as I fear our mother will not be able to rise from her bed today. You know how she is when she becomes overwrought.'

'Will Lord Bentley be very angry you have asked him for money?' Millie's face crumpled. 'I shall not come down until he has gone, please do not ask me to. I am trembling at the very thought.'

Rose was not looking forward to the meeting either but refrained from saying so. 'Of course you may stay up here. I shall tell him you are taking care of Mama. What do I do if Sir Richard arrives? Shall I have him sent away?'

Millie wrung her hands. 'I don't know, I can't think straight. I do so wish to see him, but I don't want him to know how dire our situation is. What should I do?'

'I shall take care of things. You go and sit with Mama and I shall come up and tell you what happens during the meeting.'

★ ★ ★

Perry had broken his fast and was waiting impatiently for the appearance of his sister. He wished to put in motion the making of new gowns for the Bannerman ladies. He had foregone his usual morning ride.

Had Rose missed him?

He was pacing his study when the butler appeared holding a silver salver in front of him.

'A letter has arrived by hand, your Grace. The footman did not wait for a reply but said the matter was urgent.'

'I shall be going out directly. Have my horse brought round immediately.' Perry didn't need to read the letter, he could think of only one person who would write to him in this way. His heart dropped to his boots. He tore open the sheet and read the contents. He'd known the letter would be from Rose but expected the missive to tell him she was terminating the engagement. A wave of relief engulfed him. Financial ruin? This was something he *could* deal with. His dismissal would have been far more difficult. He realized how much he wished the marriage to take place.

He quickly scribbled one letter to his lawyer asking Mr. Radcliff to attend him immediately in Grosvenor Square. A second note would go to his bank warning them he would be requiring a substantial withdrawal of funds later in the day. Satisfied he had done everything to expedite matters he strode through the house, bounded up the stairs, and headed for his apartment at the rear of the building. Ten minutes later he was astride Lucifer and heading for Grosvenor Square.

★ ★ ★

There was a feeling of apprehension pervading the house. Mama's incautious remarks had been overheard and spread below stairs. The entire staff was awaiting the arrival of Lord Bentley with as much anticipation as Rose was. Not only could the family be in the streets, but also those they employed would be homeless. She had read the letter from the bank so many times the ink was smudged. Was the mortgage referred to only on the London house or did it also include their main estate in Hertfordshire?

Clutching the wrinkled paper she sank into a chair, lent her head back and closed her eyes. She needed a few minutes to gather her wits before Perry arrived. No, she was not comfortable using his given name even in her own thoughts. He must remain Lord Bentley for the present.

She stiffened. She read the paper once more and a surge of rage replaced her anxiety. Why had she not noticed this before? The missive was not addressed to her father as it should have been, but to her *mother*. The bank could not possibly believe her mother was in a position to deal with matters. A wife had no authority in her husband's financial affairs.

Good grief! These villains must have discovered she was affianced to one of the richest men in England. Using this knowledge they had decided to terrify her mother into appealing to Lord Bentley for help. Why hadn't she read the letter more carefully? Too late to repine — the damage was done — the Duke was on his way.

Holding the meeting in her father's study would be appropriate; after all the matter they were to discuss was of a business nature. The fire was already lit. The room was pleasantly warm, although decidedly dark for the sun did not reach this side of the house until later in the day. Not bothering to summon a servant, she pushed a spill into the flames and touched it to the wicks of all the available candles.

She stared around the room, trying to make up her mind where to sit. Should she be seated at all? Coffee and pastries had already been ordered and would arrive as soon as Lord Bentley was settled. She was dithering about the chamber when he strode in. Before she could protest he gathered her into his arms.

'Sweetheart, you must not distress yourself. I shall take care of everything for you. Did I not tell you as my future bride no one will show you disrespect.' His arms tightened. He was going to kiss her again.

Pushing hard against his chest she protested. 'Please, your Grace, release me. There is something I have to tell you most urgently.'

'I beg your pardon, my love. Shall we be seated or are we to stand for this revelation?' His expression was tender, a slight smile curving his lips. He was irresistible in this teasing mode and she needed her wits about her.

'It makes no difference. Here, read this letter and tell me what you think.' She pushed the paper into his hands and retreated behind the large mahogany desk. His expression changed. He had grasped instantly what had taken her an hour to understand.

'Devil take it! Someone at the bank shall pay dearly for this.'

His eyes were hard. She was glad his fury was directed elsewhere.

'How dare they attempt to extort money from Lady Bannerman? I shall deal with this. I give you my word they will not bother you again.' He glanced in her direction. He was about to join her behind the desk when a parlour maid appeared carrying the tray of refreshments.

'Kindly put it here, Betty, I shall serve. There's no need for you to wait.' Rose busied herself pouring the coffee. 'Do you take cream in your coffee, your Grace? Sugar?'

'Neither, thank you. Nor do I require

a pastry. Kindly stop fussing and come here and sit down with me. I shall do nothing to alarm you.'

She edged cautiously from behind the desk, not sure she believed him. There was a definite gleam in his eye. His idea of what might alarm her might not correspond to hers. She picked up a cup and saucer and held them like a shield in front of her. 'Your drink is on the tray, your Grace.'

His chuckle released the tension and she risked a glance at him. He was standing no more than her hand's width in front of her. Her hand jerked and a stream of scalding coffee drenched her hand. With a squeal of anguish she dropped the cup sending the remaining contents down his breeches.

His language burnt her ears. 'I am so sorry, your Grace, I have quite spoilt your . . . '

'Heavens above, Rosamund, you are a danger to yourself and those around you. Show me your hand.'

Obediently she held it out; a pink

mark ran across her knuckles. 'I shall go at once and see to it.' She carefully avoided looking at the area of his person which was wet. 'I am sorry to have caused you injury. No doubt you will need to return to home and change.' Not waiting to hear his reply she fled from the room. This incident had just confirmed what she already knew to be true.

Somehow she would persuade him to break off the engagement. She must do something to convince him he would be making a mistake if he married her. She was quite certain he would not allow her to terminate the arrangement as matters stood.

Although a lady could break an engagement without incurring the censure of the *ton*, a gentleman could not. He had done the right thing by offering for her. When she jilted him *she* would be disgraced. He could be free of an unnecessary entanglement and able to find himself a more suitable wife.

Only as she reached the sanctuary of

her apartment did she recall the actual reason for his visit. He had said he would deal with the bank. Did this mean he would leave things as they were until Papa returned or that he would pay the mortgage? She could not let him do this for his involvement would tie her irrevocably to their betrothal.

10

With a resigned sigh Perry collected the shards of broken porcelain and placed them on the tray. His breeches were beyond help. At least the coffee had been cooler when it splattered him. If he remained on his feet and made sure his jacket tails were hanging straight then most of the stain was hidden from view. He had arranged for his lawyer to meet him here, so could hardly depart. The wet patch was deucedly uncomfortable; perhaps if he stood closer to the fire the material would dry more quickly. He must decide what action to take. He was certainly not going to pay the bank. They had no right to demand such a thing in the absence of Lord Bannerman.

He smiled grimly. He would make it his business to ruin this bank. They would not be left with the wherewithal to continue to trade by the time he had finished with them. A strong smell of damp cloth and coffee filled the room. This reminded him he had not yet drunk his own brew. He strolled across to the desk, swallowed down his cup and refilled it from the jug. Rose seemed to be permanently in the centre of some catastrophe or other. He considered what it might be like to have his well-ordered life turned upside down by her entry into it.

Suddenly the door slammed against the wall and his beloved rushed in. Her pretty gown was unchanged, her face pale and her eyes wide with something he hoped *wasn't* apprehension.

'Lord Bentley, I thought you might have left. I'm so glad you're still here, for there is something most particular I wish to say.'

He seemed unsurprised by her precipitous entry and waved her to a chair. She ignored his gesture; she was not staying long enough to require a seat.

'I thought we had decided, sweetheart, you are to call me by my given name.' His disarming smile confused her. 'However, Lord Bentley is a slight improvement on, *your Grace*, I suppose.'

'I believe we also agreed you would cease to sprinkle your conversation with unnecessary endearments, my lord.' Reluctantly her lips curved. 'I realized I had not made it clear we no longer require you to intervene on our behalf. My father will be home by the summer and will take care of things then. I'm certain he will remove his business from that particular bank immediately.'

For a second he was a formidable stranger and then the moment passed. 'Leave arrangements to me, my dear. In the absence of your father and brother I stand as head of your household. My lawyer will be arriving momentarily and will ensure Lady Bannerman will not be bothered again.'

She frowned, not sure if he had answered her question as she wished or was prevaricating. 'Will you give me your word you will not pay off the mortgages? That you will wait until my father is home before becoming financially involved with my family?'

'I promise. Now, my love, might I suggest that you return to your apartment and change your gown? I am sure you do not wish to be seen in such disarray by any visitors.'

A mischievous impulse made her curtsy as if she were indeed a child being sent to her chamber. 'Yes, sir, I shall do so at once.'

'Saucy minx, I can see I shall need to take you in hand once we are wed.' His eyes glinted. His body tensed as if he were about to pounce on her.

With more speed than dignity she rushed from the study, almost colliding with the butler and a stick-thin, black-garbed gentleman who were about to enter. She muttered an apology and fled along the passageway eager to hide her burning face. She would change her gown and see Mama and give her the good news.

Rose was obliged to put on a plain morning gown as she had spoiled her only fashionable ensemble. The only redeeming feature of this ensemble was the russet colour of the material. Millie and her mother were tearfully awaiting news of what had taken place in the library.

'At last! It has been an age since you went downstairs. What did Lord Bentley say? Will he save us from destitution or are we to be turned into the streets like beggars?'

'Mama, it would not have come to that. The bank had no right to apply directly to you. They were intending Lord Bentley would step in and pay off the mortgage. There's no need for him to do that, matters can be left until Papa returns.'

'I don't understand, Rose. Are you saying the bank could not foreclose even if Lord Bentley did not help us?'

'I am. I have thanked him for his willingness to help but made him promise not to settle anything. Far better these difficulties are dealt with by Papa and not a stranger.'

'What are you saying, you silly girl, Lord Bentley is your betrothed. He is to be my son-in-law in the autumn. He is part of our family, not a stranger.'

Fortunately Millie intervened before Rose said something she might later regret. 'Is he to escort you to the musical evening at the Benton's this evening, Rose?'

'I've no idea, we didn't discuss that. Do you wish me to go down and ask him, I don't believe he has left yet?' Her announcement sent her mother in to a spasm. The thought that such an illustrious gentleman had been abandoned so cavalierly was too much for her jangled nerves.

Rigby, their mother's dresser, shooed them out promising she could take care of her patient better in their absence. The smell of burnt feathers followed them into the passageway.

Rose clutched her sister's arm overcome by an inappropriate desire to giggle. 'I did not mean to upset her. The Duke is waiting for his legal person to attend him. I was not required to remain with him.' She laughed. 'Anyway I had to come up to change my gown because I tipped coffee all over it.'

Millie giggled and linked her arm with hers. 'That's two gowns destroyed in less than a day. My dearest, even for you, that's a record.'

'I forgot, he says I am not to go about in public until he has replaced my wardrobe. Heaven knows how long that will take.' Her sister's eyes rounded. 'Don't worry, Millie, you and Mama are to have new garments too. He was determined on it, said he had deep pockets and was pleased to spend it on his future family.'

'A complete wardrobe? For all of us? How wonderful, Richard need not be ashamed of me in future. I have been aware that we are not dressed in the first stare of fashion, country seamstresses do not produce gowns that do in the *ton*.'

Rose squeezed Millie's arm affectionately. 'I would not have applied to him today if he had not already told me he was willing to offer financial support.'

* * *

Perry rode from Grosvenor Square satisfied he had done everything necessary to protect his future wife and family. His lawyer informed him Lord Bannerman had not in fact, as rumour had it, made poor business decisions. Bannerman had taken out the mortgages in order to invest in a fleet of cargo ships. Sheer bad luck, not lack of judgement, had placed the family in financial difficulties.

He was greeted with effusion on his return. His sister had received his message and was eager to set matters in motion. 'Perry, do you wish me to send my own *modiste* to Grosvenor Square or do you have someone else in mind?'

'I shall leave matters to you, Laura. After all, you produced a triumph in a matter of hours yesterday. I am relying on you to guide Rose and her family in their choices.' He turned to his man-of-affairs who was waiting politely to speak to him. 'Well, Adams, what is it? Can't you see that I am occupied?'

Adams bowed. 'It is a matter of the utmost urgency, your Grace. A letter has come from your estate in Surrey that requires your immediate attention.'

'Very well, I shall be with you directly. Laura, it's quite possible I shall have to go out of town for a while, but I give you my word I will return in good time for your ball.'

'I should think so too. I was thinking we should perhaps make an official announcement of your betrothal at the event. Serve champagne after supper? What do you think?'

He shook his head. 'I think not, Laura. My engagement is already known. There's no need to broadcast it further, especially as Lord Bannerman is not aware his wife has given me permission to marry Rose.'

His sister looked at him as if he were a candidate for Bedlam. 'Are you suggesting, Perry, that Bannerman might refuse his consent? No father in his right mind would turn down the most eligible bachelor in the country. Good Lord, the girl will become a duchess whilst she is barely out of the schoolroom.'

'Exactly so; I'm beginning to think she is far too young to embark on matrimony. At times I am dealing with a child not a woman grown. I am uncertain she will fulfil the role of Duchess of Essex efficiently.'

'Poppycock! She will grow into the position.'

'I do not intend to marry in the autumn. I think it better if we have a long engagement and get to know each other better.' He frowned. 'I'm not sure she's ready for the responsibility of becoming my wife.'

'Are you having second thoughts, brother? I thought you head over ears in love with the chit after your performance last night on the dance floor.

Besides, you cannot cry off. Unless Miss Bannerman changes her mind you are committed.'

'I am fond of her, and will do everything in my power to keep her from harm, but as for love? I'm not sure what that is. Surely it's far better to respect and like your partner than to be entangled in a lot of emotional nonsense?'

On that note he nodded and strode off to his study to discover what had agitated Adams.

*   *   *

Lady Bannerman, on receiving the information she was to acquire an entire wardrobe at no expense, immediately recovered her spirits. 'Oh my! Are you sure, my dearest Rose, that his Grace is happy to have all bills sent to him?'

'Everything, Mama, even incidentals. Papa will think he has returned to a trio of fashionable strangers.' Rose was not entirely comfortable about the arrangement, but was relieved the Duke was not obliged to redeem Papa's debts. The expense of new gowns for them all in comparison was a mere bagatelle.

By the time the exquisite mantua maker and her helpers had departed with their measurements the clock had struck three. She drew her sister to one side.

'Millie, I must speak to you. Please come to our apartment so we might be private.'

'I will be happy to sit down after so much excitement. I've never seen so many different materials and fashion plates — I swear we shall not know ourselves when fitted out in such style.'

The fire in their parlour was burning merrily. Mary was busy so they had the place to themselves. Rose curled up in a chair, kicking off her slippers and tucking her stockinged feet under the skirt of her dress.

'Millie, I believe Lord Bentley and I are not suited. He finds me irritating and not up to his high standards and I find him dictatorial and proud.'

'Nonsense! I might have believed you if I had not seen with my own eyes the way you danced last night. Whatever reservations you might have are merely pre-wedding nerves. You two were meant to be together exactly as Richard and I are.'

When had her sister become so sensible? It would seem despite their tender years they had become adults these past few weeks.

'Then you do not think I should cry off?'

Millie's tinkling laughter filled the chamber. 'He wouldn't allow you to do so even if you wanted to. No man wishes to be jilted.' She clapped her hands. 'Imagine, dearest, his shock if he was to be turned down? Why, he is the most eligible *parti* in the country; he could marry anyone.'

'It's no laughing matter. I don't love him and I am certain he does not love me . . . '

'But, Rose, did you not say you were prepared to marry without love in order to save the family's finances? Anyway, it's too late to repine for our new clothes are ordered. We can hardly expect a gentleman quite unconnected to us to pay the bills. I'm certain we have spent a vast fortune. Papa does not have the wherewithal to pay those tradesmen so you must forget about breaking the engagement and enjoy your new status.'

Her sister was correct. Rose was committed to marrying the Duke whilst knowing he was making her his wife because he had no choice. She should never have told her mother and sister about his generous offer to replace their gowns. Was there a way out of her dilemma? How could she release him from his promise without further tarnishing both their reputations? She realised that she loved Perry too much to allow their engagement to continue. He could do so much better and her task was to find a way to release him. He might be proud, but he was perfect in every other respect

From whichever way she viewed the situation, she could come up with only one solution. She must do something so outrageous even *he* would turn against her. She could not betray him with another — that was not acceptable. No, she must come up with something else. Eventually she knew what she must do. All that was needed was the opportunity to put her plan into motion.

★　★　★

Perry restrained the urge to hurl the accounts book Adams had shown him into the fire. 'Devil take it! I suppose I must take action. How could this have happened?' He glared at his man of business. The man paled but remained resolute.

'Your factor has been with you for many years so why should you suspect him of fraud?'

'We must set off immediately. With luck we will be there before dark and the matter settled in a day or two. I do not wish to be away from town for long, my niece is having her come-out ball next week. I must be here for that.'

Unbidden, an image of Rose filled his head and he pushed it aside. Now was not the time to be thinking about her. Had he not already decided their nuptials were to be postponed, perhaps indefinitely?

'Very well, your Grace. Do you wish me to order your carriage?'

Perry nodded as he strode across the study and tugged the bell-strap. Minions were sent running in various directions to convey messages to his valet and sister. Laura opened the door of her private parlour herself.

'Must you go, Perry? Could you not let Adams sort out whatever is wrong down there?'

'Unfortunately, I must go myself. However, my dear, I shall be back in good time for the ball. Could I ask a favour of you? Would you go and see Lady Bannerman and ensure Rose is not getting into mischief in my absence.'

'Good heavens, brother, whatever do you mean? I'm quite sure your betrothed won't do anything untoward now she is allied to our family.'

'She's still scarcely more than a child. I should not be engaged to her if she had any more sense than a pea goose. As I mentioned previously, I have serious reservations about her suitability. Do I have your word you will keep an eye on her in my absence?'

'I think you do her a disservice, but I shall go round. Or I could perhaps invite her to stay for a night or two?'

'No, she has nothing suitable to wear until her new garments are made. Perhaps you could ride with her in the mornings?'

His sister shuddered delicately. 'Ride? Whatever next? You know I abhor early mornings. I shall visit tomorrow and see how things are.'

With that he had to be satisfied. As his travelling carriage rattled over the cobbles later he had ample time to consider his future. He must not allow himself to become sentimental for marriage was a business like any other. If his feelings became involved he would not be able to make sensible decisions. Rosamund Bannerman was too young and wild to make him a suitable duchess — so why did the thought of losing her depress his spirits?

11

Unwilling to go out to any public events without Lord Bentley, Rose spent the next week perfecting her plan to convince him he would be better off without her. Lady Laura Foster had visited twice and Rose had done her best to convince her ladyship she was an eccentric.

'Rose, I quite despair of you. Have you completely lost your senses, child?' Her mother looked more bewildered than annoyed. 'Since when did you become involved in philanthropic works? Good heavens, is it not enough your dear father spends far too much of our precious income on the less fortunate?'

'I am merely following his example, Mama. When I am a duchess I shall have unlimited funds available to me. Who better than I to set up a home for veterans who have given their health to protect their country?'

Rose had decided to state to all and sundry she was to become a patroness of a charity set up to help ex-servicemen. To this end she had informed her future sister-in-law Bentley Hall was the ideal place to house these men.

'I shudder to think what poor Lady Laura Foster thought of your plans. For you to suggest that the ancestral home be used in this way quite beggars belief.'

Millie giggled. 'Don't fret, Mama, it will never happen. Can you imagine the Duke of Essex allowing common folk free access to his home? Richard tells me only a select few, those in the highest echelons of society, are entertained there.'

'Very true, my love. Indeed, I am not expecting to be invited there myself. I am well aware I am far below his touch — quite definitely his social inferior. Why, he throws me into palpitations just by raising one eyebrow.'

Any desire to laugh Rose had vanished at these words. Her dearest relatives had reminded her how proud he was, how he considered himself above everyone else. This hardened her resolve to break off the engagement. She would not marry a man who found her family wanting.

'I wish Papa and David would return. I cannot feel easy about matters until we have his blessing.'

Her sister's face fell. 'Oh, Rose, do you think he might refuse his permission? We cannot marry without it, and I don't believe I could survive three years apart from my beloved.'

'Why should your papa not agree to your marrying the most eligible man in England, Rose? And as for you, Millie my darling, there can be no objection to Sir Richard, I'm sure. Even if *he* is not a rich man, Lord Bentley's settlements will pay off the creditors.'

Whichever way she looked at it Rose could see no way out of her dilemma. Unless her father returned with their fortune restored all would be lost.

'When do we expect Papa and David to arrive?'

'Not until next month at the earliest for it takes a prodigiously long time to sail from India to England. More importantly, Lady Laura Foster tells me the first of our new gowns will be arriving tomorrow morning. When Lord Bentley returns to Town I shall thank him in person.'

'He has been delayed on business and is not expected back for another day or two. Now, I have some pamphlets I wish to read. Will you excuse me please, Mama?'

She had not been long upstairs when the parlour door burst open. She was unsurprised her sister had followed her.

'Rose, what's bothering you? You've not been yourself these past few days. In fact, not since you put your foot through your gown at the Ponsonby's ball.'

'I cannot marry Lord Bentley. I'm everything he doesn't need in a wife.' Counting on each finger she listed the disadvantages of the match. 'Firstly I am far too young; he needs an older woman, not someone flighty. Secondly I am clumsy; thirdly I am too outspoken and fourthly I lack the social graces necessary to be a duchess. Finally I am not nearly pretty enough.' She waited for her sister to protest but Millie remained silent, her expression serious.

'You will not be young for ever, so that's no objection. You can learn what's necessary and are only clumsy when you're nervous. And it's nonsensical to say you're not pretty. Have you looked in the glass recently?' Millie clapped her hands and smiled. 'There, dearest, I have removed all your objections so you can marry him with a clear conscience.'

'I noticed you didn't suggest I wasn't too outspoken — do I not have to learn to hold my tongue as well as everything else?'

'No, I think Lord Bentley likes you the way you are otherwise he would not have offered for you, would he?'

Rose wanted to stamp her feet and throw a cushion across the room. 'He offered because of my stupidity. He will be as pleased as I when the engagement is dissolved.' Botheration! She had revealed her intentions.

'You are trying to give him a disgust of you . . . make him ready to release you without a fuss. Why, Rose, when you love him so much? I don't understand.'

'It's because I love him that I'm going to let him go. I believe we have been engaged long enough for my behaviour in the park to have been forgotten. Even Mama believes it to be a love match after our waltz together.' She blinked back tears as she recalled the way he'd kissed her. If she hadn't known better she might have thought he had feelings for her.

'But what if he does love you and you push him away by your behaviour? Then both of you will be miserable and all for nothing.'

'He's in no danger of falling in love with me; in fact the opposite is happening. What affection there was at the outset is rapidly diminishing as he gets to know me better. I shall break the engagement when he returns. I shall be the guilty party and retire to the country in disgrace.'

'But . . . '

Rose turned away unable to continue the conversation. 'Please, Millie, say no more about this. I'm going to write some letters to members of the government protesting at the inhuman treatment of the returning veterans. With any luck I shall offend so many important gentlemen Lord Bentley will wish to strangle me when he returns.'

'I shall say nothing else on the subject, my love. But I do wish you had chosen widows and orphans as your cause and not rough soldiers and sailors. I am expecting to find a queue of unsavoury characters in the stable yard as word gets out of your interest.'

This was not an aspect of her plan that she had considered. The idea appealed to her. 'Good heavens! Imagine Mama's reaction if that was to take place? I shall go down to the kitchen and warn Cook to have bread and cheese ready to hand out to any who should knock.'

Her sister retreated to the music room knowing her protests would fall on deaf ears. By the time afternoon tea was ready in the drawing-room Rose had five letters waiting to be delivered. Her impertinence was bound to annoy the recipients and with luck the Duke would hear of her misdemeanours on his return to London.

She was rather dreading the inevitable encounter for he would be furious, and rightly so. However, she would take her dressing down meekly and then hand back his jewels. He had not returned the ring for this item was still at a fashionable jewellers being resized. Much better she had never worn this. The engagement appeared less official without having had it on her finger.

★ ★ ★

At the crack of dawn she was down-stairs heading for the yard. Her early-morning gallop around the park would help her forget her heartbreak. Orion was dancing on the cobbles, the stable boy finding it difficult to control her.

'Enough nonsense, my girl, you will damage a tendon if you continue like this.' Rose ran her gloved hand down the mare's neck and immediately she calmed.

Tom was holding the reins of Bruno, the gelding he was to ride to accompany her. He grinned and touched his cap. 'Can't think what's got into her, miss. All over the place today she is. Nothing a good gallop won't cure, though.'

'Stand still, Orion, I cannot mount with you cavorting like this.' The mare threw up her head and danced back-wards sending Rose crashing beneath the plunging feet of the bay gelding.

★   ★   ★

Perry kicked shut the study door and flung his top-coat, gloves and beaver onto a chair. He ground his teeth as he strode to the sideboard and poured himself a generous measure of cognac. He'd dropped in at his club to catch up on the *on dits* he had missed whilst in the country sorting out the mess his corrupt factor had left. Instead of having a quiet drink and a chat to his cronies though, he found himself waylaid by several irate members. These gentlemen had received letters from Rose demanding they did something for the servicemen returning to this country after the defeat of the upstart Napoleon.

What was she thinking of? He was certain she had never shown the slightest interest in this subject until now. No doubt Laura would give him a bear garden jaw tomorrow as well for neglecting his betrothed and allowing her to upset half the members of the Cabinet. He would go round to Grosvenor Square in the morning. By the time he had finished Rose would regret her interference in matters that were not her concern.

He drained his glass and refilled it, thoughtfully watching the amber liquid swirl round the crystal. Devil take it! He was a slow top tonight. Rose was no more interested in ex-servicemen than she was in entering a nunnery. He would not let her get away with it. His anger was replaced by something else. He felt as if a stone had lodged heavily in his chest. Rose wished to break off the engagement and this was her way of making sure he would be happy to acquiesce. His mouth curved. She was an original. He could think of no other young lady of his acquaintance who would come up with such a brilliant, but hare brained, scheme. He stretched out on the sofa cradling the glass and wishing he held *her* as close to his heart.

Nothing she could do would push him away. Rose was the woman he'd been waiting for all his life. For some reason she did not wish to marry him, and that alone made her unique. Through all his life he'd been denied nothing. Anything he wanted had been his for the taking and now a slip of a girl — with the most amazing violet eyes — had decided to refuse him. Tomorrow he would join her when she left for her early morning ride. He would charm and tease her into changing her mind. At no point would he frighten her again with his love making, show her how much he cared — that could wait until they were married and she was more used to having him around.

He left instructions with his valet he was to be roused at six o'clock and Lucifer was to be waiting outside at six thirty. He patted his waistcoat pocket. Snugly hidden there was the betrothal ring which he intended to place on her finger the next day.

* * *

Lucifer sidled and danced, his huge hooves sparking on the cobbles. The nearer they got to Grosvenor Square the more his stallion misbehaved. 'Steady, boy. I'm as eager as you to see my lady but I have no wish for us to suffer injury in our haste to be there.'

The horse needed no guidance to turn into the stable yard, and he entered just in time to see Orion swing her hind quarters, knocking Rose to the cobbles. She disappeared under the plunging feet of the groom's horse. He vaulted from the saddle and threw himself down expecting to see the girl he loved crushed and bleeding . . .

* * *

Rose curled into a ball as she fell and rolled safely beneath Bruno to scramble up unhurt the other side. She clutched a stirrup leather and stared down in astonishment as a figure appeared at her feet, his face ashen.

'Lord Bentley, whatever are you

doing down there? Did you take a tumble too?'

He straightened to stand, glowering, obviously not at all pleased to see her. 'God in His heaven, Rose, you could have been killed.'

'As you can see I suffered no harm, although I fear my hat will never be the same again.' The item was hanging drunkenly over one eye, the once jaunty feather snapped in half.

His lopsided grin melted something inside her. 'Let me adjust it for you, sweetheart.' Instead of straightening the object he deftly removed the pins and tossed it over one shoulder. 'It will fly off anyway once we reach the park.'

Lucifer was nuzzling Orion and her mare was enjoying every moment of his attention. 'Now I know why she was so agitated. This mishap is entirely your fault, my lord.' She patted Bruno and walked round to her own mount, presenting her left leg. 'Now the excitement is over, shall we depart?'

He threw her into the saddle with

more force than was strictly necessary. Oh dear, he *was* still annoyed. Perhaps she should not have teased him about causing the accident. Then she remembered he had far greater reason to be angry. Not waiting for him to mount she clicked her tongue and trotted out into the street. She would postpone the reckoning as long as she could. She wasn't going to miss her morning gallop even for the Duke of Essex. He could hardly berate her in public so she was safe until they returned to Grosvenor Square. Lucifer drew alongside but she kept her eyes fixed firmly ahead; she dare not look for fear of what she might see.

They had been jogging for a while when he eventually broke the silence. 'Look at me, Rose. I don't care to view the back of your head.' His voice was soft, no hint of anger.

She risked a glance sideways. Her heart thudded heavily, she couldn't look away. With infinite slowness he reached out a gloved hand and gently brushed an errant strand of hair from her eyes. His touch was so gentle she scarcely felt it.

'I have your ring here, my love; I shall give it to you before I leave.'

This was not going as it should. Why wasn't he cold and distant? Jilting him would be impossible whilst he was like this. She had no choice. She must do something else to annoy him and make him forget the accident in the stable yard. She must remind him of her impertinence to the most senior members of the government.

'I don't want the ring. I'm not ready to be married and especially not to you. You must keep it for someone more suitable.' There, she'd said it. Crouching over her mare's foam flecked neck she urged the animal faster and faster. Galloping might ease the pain.

Inch by inch he closed the gap but this time he didn't allow her to race beside him. Instead, he stretched out and grabbed her reins, bringing both animals to a rearing halt. Before she could take evasive action he lifted her from the saddle and dropped her to the grass. Her knees buckled and she sank ignominiously in a heap of blue velvet at his feet.

Tom arrived but hesitated, not sure if he should interfere. 'Here, take the horses and walk them. I shall call you when we wish to return.' The Duke stared down at her his expression pensive. 'Do you intend to sit there for much longer, my dear? I wish to talk to you and I think it better if we were alone, don't you?'

She couldn't speak; her words seemed stuck behind her teeth and her legs refused to unfold.

'Up you come.' He scooped her from the ground and set her on her feet. 'I think the small copse ahead would be ideal for our purpose, don't you?'

Her arm was threaded through his as if they were strolling around the ball-room at the Ponsonby's and, willy-nilly, she was marched towards the trees.

12

Rose's trepidation was soon replaced by anger. She was almost running in an effort to keep up! She refused to be dragged across the park like a recalcitrant schoolchild. She threw her weight backwards, digging in her heels, and he was obliged to release his hold on her arm. Bracing herself for his tirade, Rose glared up at him. 'Whatever you have to say to me, sir, can be said right here and right now.' She gestured at the empty parkland that surrounded them. 'I do not believe we are either observed or overheard.'

Instead of demanding she did as he bid, he sighed loudly. 'If you insist, my love. As you know I'm always ready to obey your instructions.'

This was doing it too brown. What was he up to now? 'Fiddlesticks to that, sir, you listen to me as much as you do your horse.' His smile was her undoing. 'I shall not apologise, so don't ask me to.' She stuck out her chin and forced her mouth into a thin line; he must not know how he affected her.

'I would not dream of asking you to, dear girl. Why should I object if you poke a stick into a hornet's nest and upset the most important gentlemen in the government? Heavens above! There's nothing I like better than being accosted by a bevy of furious politicians and having my evening ruined.' His bland tone did not fool her for one minute. He was leading up to something and she was most disconcerted not knowing what he would do next.

She tapped her foot, the sound loud in the morning silence, and tried to look unconcerned. 'Well, my lord, if you have something pertinent to say, kindly say it. I do not have all morning to stand here.' His eyes changed colour, she had struck a nerve and wished she had held her tongue.

'I wonder,' he said as he looked

round, 'I wonder if I should turn you across my knee right here or go somewhere a little more secluded.'

She swallowed and stepped backwards. 'I would much prefer it, your Grace, if you didn't do it at all.' She would not beg his forgiveness. If he had decided to chastise her in this way then nothing she could say would deflect him.

He raised his arm. She did not flinch. Finger by finger he removed his gloves. His eyes held her captive, and her knees began to tremble. Then, instead of manhandling her he held out his hand as if in supplication. She couldn't help herself. She stepped closer and placed her own in his. His fingers closed; she felt his strength, his warmth, but his hold was gentle.

'My darling, I would no sooner raise a hand to you, or any other woman, than cut my own throat. I apologise if I frightened you. I did not expect you to take me seriously.'

Somehow she found herself within

his embrace but could not remember moving.

'Perry, please, we are in full view of Tom and anyone else who might be riding in the park this morning.'

'Surely a young lady with such disregard for protocol and etiquette can have no objection to her future husband kissing her?'

His arms tightened. Her feet left the ground and a strange light-headed sensation all but overwhelmed her common sense. She must not let him do this. Drawing back her foot she lashed out. When her boot connected with his shin it had the desired effect and with a startled oath he dropped her. This gave her time to turn tail and race for the comparative safety of Tom and their mounts.

Her groom must have witnessed the whole for he was standing ready to toss her into the saddle when she arrived breathless at his side. 'Leave Lucifer. Drop his reins, he will not stray far.'

Moments after kicking the Duke of

Essex she was galloping in the opposite direction. When they reached the main thoroughfare she realized the stallion was still with them. Injuring the Duke was one thing, leaving him to walk home quite another.

'Tom, you must take Lucifer back to his Grace. I shall continue to Grosvenor Square. I shall come to no harm at this time of the morning.'

However each time he attempted to lead the stallion away from her mare he reared and lashed out. 'He won't budge, miss. I reckon as we'll have to take him with us.'

'No, I'll take him back myself.' There was no need to take Lucifer's reins, he followed her mare willingly. Rose wished that love for *her* could tame his master in the same way. He was fond of her, perhaps found her desirable, but love her he did not.

In the distance she saw him striding across the turf and for a second considered turning back. She should not have kicked him; he was a gentleman. If she'd asked him to release her he would have done so immediately. Why was it she behaved so abominably when in his vicinity?

He saw her and stopped. To her surprise he raised a hand in greeting as if pleased to see her, not furious with her as she had expected. When she was within hailing distance he called.

'Thank you for coming back, my dear. These are new boots and decidedly uncomfortable.'

'I had no choice. Lucifer would not return without my mare. He is infatuated.'

A wry smile curved his lips and his eyes danced. 'I've always said such emotions are dangerous. See how my magnificent stallion is humbled by your pretty grey mare.' He vaulted into the saddle and guided his horse to her side. 'Shall we return home? I, for one, have had more than enough excitement before I have breakfasted.'

'I'm sorry I kicked you . . . '

'Apology accepted. I should not have

tried to kiss you. I gave you my word I would not do so.' His expression changed. 'I'm sure you agree, my dear, an excess of emotion of any kind can only lead to disaster. I believe we agreed a marriage based on affection, respect and mutual interests has far more chance of success than one in which emotions are involved.'

She ought to invite him to breakfast at Grosvenor Square but she had no wish to be alone with him. His words had crushed her happiness. He was so astute he would know at once she was distressed. She had no intention of burdening him with her secret. He would be embarrassed to know she loved him and it would make it so much harder to break off the arrangement.

They were at the entrance to the stable yard, a perfect time to say what must be said. She drew rein and turned in the saddle. This was the most difficult thing she had ever done in her life.

'I agree, your Grace, but I believe we do not have even *those* things in this relationship. We are too different. Even if I wished to marry you, which I don't, I am unsuited to the position of Duchess of Essex. Therefore I am releasing you from the arrangement. My father will repay you for the money you have spent on my family's behalf. I shall be retiring to the country so you have no need to fear we will meet again.'

Blinded by tears she kicked Orion and the mare shot forward, almost unseating her. Tumbling from the saddle, she picked up her skirts and raced for the house. She was too overwrought to worry about his reaction. Fortunately the side door was ajar. She sped in, aware of the shocked faces of the two parlour maids who were busy dusting the ceiling. She hesitated at the foot of the stairs. She could not return to her apartment as Millie would still be there. The study — she would be private there, and away from prying eyes.

The room was cold. No fire had been lit today, but she was warmly dressed and would come to no harm for an hour or two. Throwing her whip and gloves onto the nearest chair she paced the carpet, angrily brushing away the moisture from her cheeks with the back of her hand. The first part of her plan was done. All that remained was to tell her mother and face the nervous hysterics her news would bring.

She watched rain drops trickle down the window pane. He would get wet on his return. She wished it had held off until he was safe inside. A slight sound behind her made her turn. Her vision blurred. A strange noise, like water rushing through a mill wheel, filled her head and darkness overwhelmed her.

* * *

Perry caught her as she crumpled. He swore under his breath at his idiocy. He had not meant to scare Rose into a fit of the vapours. He stood with his

219

precious bundle held to his chest knowing he should call for help, but reluctant to release her.

She was stirring; he'd better put her down before she came round. He carefully placed her on the sofa then snatched off his riding coat and stuffed it under her head. The room was damn cold. There was no fire ready in the grate and it would be better to employ his coat as a cover than a pillow. He was in the process of remedying this, one hand cradling her head the other holding his coat, when her eyes opened.

'Lie still, sweetheart; you fainted. I shall ring for your mother . . . '

Her vision cleared and she struggled to sit up. 'Please, don't do that.' She rubbed her eyes and shook her head, then swung her feet to the floor. 'And I did not faint . . . '

His hateful chuckle filled the room. 'No, of course you didn't, my love. I expect you were overcome with fatigue and fell asleep unexpectedly.'

'I've never fainted in my life. Since I

made your acquaintance, sir, any manner of extraordinary things have happened to me. Don't you see we are not good for each other? Do you wish me to be fainting every five minutes?'

'Don't be a ninny hammer. Why should this one occasion herald such a decline in your health? No, don't get up, I shall send for refreshments. We have much to discuss and might as well do it here even though it's a trifle chilly.'

This was the outside of enough. This was her house, *he* could not issue orders in this way. She pushed his coat to one side and jumped up, dodging nimbly past his outstretched hand, only to find she wasn't as well as she'd thought. Her head spun as she fell back and clutched a handful of his shirt to steady herself.

'Silly girl, sit down again until you feel more the thing.' Gently he guided her back to the sofa. Her legs were behaving as if she was an ancient matron not a young lady. She did feel decidedly odd; she closed her eyes and leant back. What harm could there be in allowing him to send for breakfast?

From what seemed like a distance she heard him issuing orders. A few minutes later a clatter and rattle indicated the fire was being prepared. She relaxed. Having someone taking care of her for a change was rather pleasant. Since David and Papa had left last year it had been *she* who looked out for everyone else. Mama was excellent at taking care of her own needs but tended to forget everyone else, including her own daughters.

Soon welcome warmth banished the chill and she no longer needed the comfort of his coat. She thought she must have dozed; there was no sound. He had left her to rest. She yawned and sat up to find him sitting no more than an arm's length from her. His expression was tender as if he really cared for her welfare. On a side table stood a laden tray. The delicious aroma of strong coffee and hot chocolate wafted in her direction. Her stomach gurgled loudly.

'Excellent, I'm glad you're hungry. Which would you prefer, coffee or chocolate?'

His matter-of-fact approach calmed her and she smiled apologetically. 'I haven't eaten since yesterday morning, small wonder I fainted. I apologise for blaming you.'

'I have broad shoulders, my love. I'm quite happy to accept the blame for everything untoward that has occurred since we met.'

'Now you're being ridiculous. I believe someone clever and famous once said '*an individual is the master of their own downfall*' or something equally profound. I believe I can accept full responsibility for putting my foot through my gown and behaving appallingly on numerous occasions. However I shall allow you to accept responsibility for my fainting. You have a tendency to creep up on a person in a most unexpected way.'

He handed her a bowl of chocolate and placed a plate of buns and pastries beside her on a small table. 'I do apologise for creeping — not a gentlemanly pastime, small wonder you fainted.' He grinned and tossed her a damask napkin. 'Now, stop talking nonsense and eat your breakfast.'

In companionable silence they demolished the food and drank chocolate and coffee. Eventually replete she brushed away the crumbs and wiped her mouth and sticky fingers. 'That was exactly what I needed. I expect we raised a few eyebrows skulking in here rather than going to the breakfast parlour.'

'Not at all. Everything appeared as ordered and in good time.'

She smiled. 'Good heavens! They would not dare show their surprise to someone as august as you. You can be quite sure they are, at this very moment, tittle-tattling about our strange behaviour.'

'Shall we not discuss the staff? We have far more pertinent things to talk about.' He raised his hand as she drew breath to protest. 'For once you will remain silent and listen. Is that quite clear?'

A peculiar glint in his eyes made her hesitate and she swallowed her sharp retort. He leant forward. She could feel his breath on her cheek and pressed back against the sofa.

'Excellent. I see you have remembered I am the Duke of Essex and must not be interrupted by anyone less important than myself.'

He was not serious but poking fun at himself. This would not have happened a few short weeks ago. Nodding solemnly she placed a finger on her lips and raised her brows enquiringly.

'Finally I have achieved the impossible. I never thought to see you either biddable or quiet.' He smiled sweetly and waved his hand. 'Please don't spoil things now. I have things to say and you must listen to me.'

His expression changed from playful to serious. 'Rose, I know why you wrote those letters, and it won't wash, my dear. Whatever you say to the contrary you will make me an excellent wife. Admittedly it would be better if you were older, had more experience of life, but that can't be helped. What you don't know you'll soon learn. I have no wish to go back on the marriage mart and search for someone else. You will not get a better offer and by marrying me you will be helping your family.'

'I have no wish to be married. I told you that. I don't like going to parties and balls, I much prefer to be in the countryside. I . . . '

'Then we shall live in Kent. I too would rather have my teeth pulled than attend fashionable events in Town. I have a brig moored in Dover and we can spend a year or two exploring the continent. You would love Italy; the light and colour would suit your personality.'

He made no mention of love; was she expecting too much from him? He was fond of her, took care of her and they dealt well together most of the time.

Any girl in the land would consider this a union made in heaven.

'I don't wish to wear your ring until my father has returned and given his blessing. If he agrees, then I will marry you, but not until next year. I think it better we get to know each other before embarking on a lifetime commitment.'

'A wise decision. I find it hard to accept you're not even eighteen years of age, for you are mature beyond your years.' He reached into his waistcoat pocket and withdrew the small velvet box. 'I shall leave this with you; put it with the other items. It's my niece's come-out ball the day after tomorrow. My sister had hoped to announce our betrothal as well, but I'm prepared to wait if that's what you want.'

They stood. He made no attempt to touch her and she wasn't sure if she was disappointed or relieved. After a few more banalities he departed, leaving the small box on the side table. He appeared sanguine about his choice and her reasons for refusing him had been dealt with. Would it be so very hard to marry a man she was head over ears in love with when her feelings were not reciprocated in full? A warm glow spread from toes to crown. She was committed and the thought of being his wife one day filled her with happiness. If he was satisfied she would make him a suitable duchess, then who was she to quibble?

13

The next day a stream of interesting boxes began to arrive at Grosvenor Square. For the first time in her life Rose was as excited as her sister and mother to delve into the parcels and examine the contents. There were morning gowns, promenade dresses, reticules, gloves and slippers galore.

'My word, I swear we shall be the smartest ladies in London this season. Do look at this, girls, I've never seen anything so beautiful. I'd no idea the puce satin would make up so well.'

Rose exchanged speaking looks with her sister. 'I'm sure everyone will notice your ensemble, Mama, especially with the matching turban and three egret feathers.'

'I shall wear it tomorrow night. Have you discovered your ball gowns? I should like to see them before I begin my morning calls.'

Millie held up an enchanting gown in palest damask rose silk. 'Here is mine, Mama. The over skirt of sarcenet and the little rosebuds around the hem and neckline are quite exquisite. Show us which of your choices has been completed for tomorrow, Rose.'

Sadly Rose shook her head. 'Mine does not appear to have come. I am disappointed my silver and violet gown hasn't been completed.' She held up a delightful evening gown with a demi-train. 'I shall wear this instead. The forget-me-not blue spangles are so pretty I'm sure nobody will notice it's not actually a ball gown.'

'You cannot dance in that; you will trip over your train. Heavens above, child, didn't you put your foot through your last gown and that didn't even have a train?'

Millie pulled a face behind their mother's back taking the sting out of the words. A bevy of chambermaids, headed by Mary and Rigby, began to gather up the items to take them upstairs.

By the time the drawing-room was cleared, Rose had recovered her equilibrium and was able to answer without showing how her mother's careless comment had hurt.

'Dancing with Lord Bentley there's no danger that even I, clumsy as I am, will trip over anything, Mama. Have no fear, I shall not embarrass you tomorrow.'

Their mama departed leaving Rose to talk to her sister. 'I was so looking forward to tomorrow. I wanted to look my very best. I hope I don't disappoint him when I appear inappropriately dressed.'

'You repine too much, dearest. I have noticed at least a third of all the women are in evening wear, not ball gowns. That blue gown is stunning — even lovelier than the silver. You will look beautiful and well you know it.'

'Thank you, you have restored my confidence. Still, it's strange my gown didn't arrive when we had made it perfectly clear I should need it tomorrow.' She wandered to the window and looked out. 'It's a lovely morning; shall we walk to the park? I cannot bear to be cooped up inside today. I know I have already ridden this morning but I am far too restless to remain here.'

'Richard is coming to take me for a drive. I would ask you to accompany us . . .'

'I wouldn't dream of doing so, my love. I shall take Mary and a footman and go for a walk on my own. No, do not raise your eyebrows at me. It's perfectly proper for a young lady to promenade when accompanied by her abigail and a male member of staff.' She giggled. 'Anyway, it's a good excuse to wear one of my new ensembles. Which one are you going to change into?'

Half an hour later she was smartly dressed in a lavender velvet pelisse, matching gown and half-kid boots. Rose tied the ribbons of the pretty bonnet which completed her outfit.

'There, Millie, I daresay even Mama would not recognize me now.' She scowled at her booted toes peeping from beneath the hem of her gown. 'These are decidedly uncomfortable and I'm tempted to put on my old ones.'

A double shriek of horror at her suggestion made her laugh. Neither her sister nor her maid would hear of her spoiling the look of her new ensemble by wearing anything but the matching footwear.

Sir Richard arrived as she was leaving and his stunned expression was worth the aggravation of pinched toes. She curtsied and he bowed deeply.

'I say, Miss Rose, you look absolutely splendid. I scarcely recognized you.' He was bemused by her delighted chuckle.

'Millie will be ready in a moment, sir; I hope you have a pleasant excursion. Shall you be going to the park?'

He nodded.

'Then I might well see you, as that is where I'm headed too.'

Still smiling she ran lightly down the steps and out onto the footpath. Her appearance caused an unfortunate young gentleman to miss his footing. He stumbled into the road narrowly avoiding being crushed by a passing carriage. How unfair that beautiful clothes should change the way one was viewed, but nevertheless admiration was a most enjoyable and novel experience.

Although it was scarcely a mile to the park she was bitterly regretting her decision long before she reached her destination. Her toes were sadly crushed. She feared she would never walk normally again. 'Mary, I must find somewhere to sit down. Perhaps if I take off these wretched boots . . . '

'You must not do that, miss, not in a public place. Look, there are the gates just ahead. I remember seeing a bench or two by the ornamental flower beds.'

Gritting her teeth Rose marched on, every step a torture. She had never been more grateful in her life to see a marble bench. She doubted she would be able to walk back without hobbling like an old crone.

Once seated, she turned her mind to the problem. There was only one solution which presented itself. Fred, the footman, must return to the house and fetch the carriage. Then she recalled Millie and Sir Richard would be arriving soon. 'Fred, if you wait by the main thoroughfare, do you think you would recognize Sir Richard's carriage?'

'I will, Miss Rose. I'll wave him down all right. Will I fetch him over?'

'No, just tell him of my predicament and ask Miss Bannerman to arrange for the carriage to be sent when she returns home. I shall be perfectly content sitting here; there's no need for them to curtail their excursion.'

She had not been sitting long when she heard a strange sound coming from the clipped shrubs that boarded the garden. 'Mary, do you hear that? Is it a child crying over there?'

'I reckon it might be, I'll go over and look.'

Bored by her enforced idleness Rose decided to investigate herself. Her feet did not hurt nearly so badly after sitting down. 'I shall accompany you. I can't imagine why there should be a lost child here as this is not a place nursemaids bring their charges.'

Without a second's hesitation she dropped to her knees in the dirt and parted the branches. Instead of seeing an urchin's face she saw a shaggy dog, trapped fast by his matted fur. 'Oh, you poor thing. Quickly, Mary, we must release him. See, he's so weak; he must have been here for days.'

* * *

Perry was driven from his home by the chaos caused by the preparations for the grand ball the following day. He decided to call at Grosvenor Square. Laura had said the first of the new garments would be arriving today. He would like to see what his blunt had been spent on. He had an appointment at his lawyers later that afternoon so decided he would use his carriage. When he stepped out he saw Richard leading Millie towards his own vehicle. 'Good morning, Miss Bannerman, Devonshire. I trust I see you both well?' From the elegance of the young lady's attire he realized he was observing one of his purchases. The girl looked quite stunning — not as lovely as Rose, but she certainly dressed to advantage.

'Lord Bentley, Rose is not here. She has gone for a walk in the park. I'm sure if you go that way you will see her.' She smiled confidingly. 'I expect she would be glad to be driven home for her new boots are not as comfortable as she'd hoped.'

'In which case, Miss Bannerman, I shall go at once to her rescue.' Grinning at his friend, he nodded and leapt back into his carriage. His coachman had overheard and needed no instructions.

Minutes later the vehicle bowled through the gates. He banged on the roof and it rocked to a standstill. 'I shall proceed on foot. Jenkins, you'll need to stay alert and be ready to turn the carriage if needs be.'

Where would his beloved go? This was a vast park and busy with walkers, riders and carriages. 'Excuse me, your Grace, I believe Miss Bannerman is in the flower garden.' From his vantage point on the box the coachman had obviously seen what he could not, as his view was blocked by the vehicle. Perry stepped around and his jaw dropped. Sure enough there was Rose — it could be none other — on her knees in the mud whilst dressed in one of her new outfits. What the devil was she doing?

★ ★ ★

'Miss Bannerman, it's the Duke; he don't look too pleased neither.'

'Mary, he's a godsend. I cannot release the poor creature on my own.' She scrambled to her feet and ran to meet him. 'Perry, I am so glad to see you. There's a dog trapped in the bushes. I cannot get him out, he's stuck fast.'

'Show me. I have my carriage nearby, Jenkins will have what we need if I cannot do it myself.' He dropped to his knees as oblivious of his immaculate unmentionables as she had been of her new gown. 'Well then, old fellow, I'll soon have you free. Good boy, lie still, your ordeal is almost over.' His reached in and wrenched the branches apart. 'Quickly, darling, pull him out. I cannot hold these back for long.'

The dog was scarcely more than a puppy. He licked her hand feebly and his plumy tale wagged just once. 'Poor little thing, you must be so hungry and thirsty. I shall take you home and make you better.' The animal weighed nothing in her arms for he was hair and bones, no substance at all. She held him close, willing him to survive.

'Give him to me, sweetheart, he will be vermin-infested . . . '

She shook her head. 'I don't care; it's far too late to worry about such things.'

She turned to carry the puppy towards the waiting carriage and stumbled. Immediately his arm encircled her waist.

'In which case, I shall carry both of you. I gather your new boots are not to your liking.'

Astonished by his perspicacity she forgot to admonish him for his definite breach of protocol. An interested crowd of spectators had gathered to witness this unusual happening. Rose hid her face in his collar, her face hot with embarrassment. Unperturbed by the spectacle he was creating, he lowered his head and whispered conspiratorially in her ear.

'I believe we will be the subject of dinner table conversation again this evening, sweetheart. I doubt anyone has seen a duke with a young lady in his arms who is herself carrying a flea-infested stray. They will think us both touched in the attic.'

If he could find humour in the situation then she must be braver. She raised her head, smiling up at him. 'I doubt there's a gentleman in London who would do as you are. I cannot think why I ever thought you proud. I could not find a kinder or more generous husband if I were to search for ever.'

His arms tightened and the dog whimpered in protest; immediately he slackened his grip and increased his pace. The under coachman was standing at the steps ready to offer his assistance. Perry ducked his head and stepped in depositing her, and her precious burden, on one side and folding his lean length in the other. The carriage was in motion almost before she had time to draw breath.

'Good heavens! We have forgotten Mary and Fred.' He raised an eyebrow in query.

'My maid and footman; I have abandoned them in the park.'

'I should think on balance, my dear girl, they would much prefer to walk home than be closeted in here with that miserable object. He is distinctly malodorous as well as having crawlers the size of cockroaches.'

Rose giggled. 'I fear you're right. I have a distinct tendency to ruin the beautiful clothes you give me. I wish you had seen me when I set out. My finery caused several gentlemen to miss their step.'

His smile sent her pulse rocketing. 'I'm not surprised, even in your disarray you are quite lovely.' His expression changed; he pressed himself back into the corner where she couldn't see his face. He obviously regretted his remark and had spoken without thought, not something he was wont to do.

There was no time to dwell on this as she must concentrate on her charge. Her mother would forbid her to bring the animal in the house. With luck she would be able to smuggle him in before he was discovered. The carriage halted and the door was opened promptly. Before she could protest Perry removed the creature from her arms and gently propelled her down the steps, which were raised immediately she stepped down. The carriage door shut and she was left standing on the pavement whilst he drove away with her dog. He must have planned this with his coachman. He had never intended she take the dog in.

Ignoring the startled glances of a matron and her daughter who chose that moment to walk by, she hobbled up the steps and in through the open door. Collapsing on a convenient chair she unhooked her boots and threw them unceremoniously across the hallway. Symonds remained impassive, merely pointing whilst a boot boy ran and fetched the offending objects. It would be some time before Mary returned to help her disrobe and Rose needed to remove the garments forthwith before she spread fleas about the house. Symonds sucked his tooth loudly.

'You'll be wanting a bath, then, Miss Rose?'

'I will, thank you. Have Daisy sent

up, she can take care of me until Mary returns.'

The offending garments had been safely removed for laundering and she was bathed and reading quietly in her sitting room when Millie bounced back. Her sister had heard nothing of her exploits and sat wide-eyed whilst Rose explained.

'Lord Bentley has taken your stray dog away? How sad, he might have had a chance if you kept him here.'

'Millie, he will not harm my pet; he will take care of him for me. He has taken the dog in order to save me the inconvenience. It's far better the little chap is with him than here upsetting Mama.'

Her sister shook her head in bewilderment. 'The more I know about Lord Bentley the less I understand him. Did he not cavil at you ruining your expensive outfit? I believe that even my dear Richard might complain if I did something so extraordinary.'

'That's why I am marrying Lord

Bentley and you are marrying Sir Richard. Now, I believe I heard Mary returning. She will be agog to know what happened.'

A discreet knock on the door proved she was mistaken. A footman entered with another dressmaker's box in his arms. 'Miss Bannerman, this has arrived for you. The girl apologised and said this had been sent to the wrong address.'

Millie clapped her hands. 'Your missing gown. Open it immediately, I wish to see if it is as lovely as the last one.'

'No, I shall not look now. I shall wait until tomorrow night and then it shall be a surprise for both of us.'

*   *   *

That night she lay awake thinking about Perry's comment. From whichever way she viewed it she could come to only one conclusion — something so wonderful, so unlikely, she could scarcely credit it. The only possible explanation was he had fallen in love with her. Why else would he have called her beautiful when she knew she was not? Only a gentleman in love would be so blind to her obvious imperfections. She hugged this knowledge to her heart; she couldn't wait to see him the next morning. She would not embarrass him by mentioning his slip. Time enough for him to tell her how he felt when Papa was back and they were officially engaged. Perry was certain to be there to accompany her on her ride tomorrow morning. He would know she would be anxious to have news of the stray they had saved between them.

14

Rose was dressed and on her way to the stables just after seven o'clock the next morning. She was bubbling with excitement. Perry would be there to ride with her. Symonds waylaid her as she reached the bottom of the stairs holding out a silver tray.

'This arrived a moment ago, Miss Rose, a smart looking cove brung it — never waited for no reply.'

She removed the letter and nodded her thanks. The note was from Perry, she'd recognized the black scrawl at once. She stepped across so the light from the long window by the front door fell upon the missive.

My dearest girl,
I cannot ride with you this morning and I know that you will have been expecting me. Unfortunately however,

business matters detain me.

I cannot wait until this evening; do not forget you are engaged to dine with us at six o'clock.

The puppy is much better, and now he is bathed and vermin free I could almost like him. His coat is grey. Indeed, sweetheart, he so resembles a mop head that I have decided to name him Mop. I hope that meets with your approval.

When he is well enough he shall come to you. I'm quite certain Lady Bannerman will be overjoyed to make his acquaintance.

I shall expect you to wear your betrothal ring & as much of the Bentley jewellery as you wish.

I remain yours

The letter was signed with the indecipherable squiggle that could be his given name or something else entirely. If the curmudgeonly footman had not been hovering across the vestibule watching her she would have kissed the paper and pressed it to her bosom. She loved him so much, especially his sense of fun. She pursed her lips as she re-read his demand she wear the ring. In time she would become accustomed to his dictatorial manner. Pushing the paper into the pocket of her riding habit she continued to the side door and out into the stable yard. Even Orion was subdued this morning; her mare missed the company of Perry's stallion as much as she missed his master.

★ ★ ★

Rose and her sister were curled up comfortably in armchairs in front of a roaring fire in the small drawing-room when their mother returned from her morning calls. She sailed in and immediately began her tirade.

'Rose, what is it about you that is so determined to draw unwelcome attention to this family? What were you thinking of, child, to be scrabbling around in the dirt after a mangy cur? How could you think to involve Lord Bentley in your nonsense? I have been told by three separate acquaintances of your extraordinary behaviour.'

'If the Duke of Essex has no complaint then I am content. I beg your pardon if you have been embarrassed, but I answer to my future husband. He sent me a note to say the little dog is progressing well, and to tell you that we are to dine with them before the ball.'

This was a timely reminder and distracted her mother immediately. 'I had quite forgot. Good heavens, girls, why are you sitting here reading when you should be getting ready? It's already almost four o'clock. Run along immediately, you must both look your best. Millie, my love, is Sir Richard to join us here?'

'He is. I hope you don't mind if he travels in our carriage?'

'Of course not, he's the most charming gentleman and not given to eccentric behaviour, as are others I could mention.' She sniffed loudly and dabbed her eyes with a lace handkerchief. 'If only your dear papa was here he would know what to do. I have grave doubts about your betrothal, Rosamond. Lord Bentley might be a duke but he is decidedly peculiar and a bad influence on you. If he was not so rich, and in a position to save the family from destitution, I do declare I would have your father forbid the marriage.'

Rose was on her feet and her book tumbled to the floor unnoticed. 'I shall marry him and nothing you and Papa shall say will dissuade me. I will hear no more criticism; he is the kindest and most generous of men. Are you not wearing a gown that *he* paid for?'

Her mother's face turned an unbecoming shade of red. 'You forget yourself, miss. I am your mother and you will speak to me with respect or I shall have you locked in your bedroom.'

'Mama, you will get a sick headache if you continue to upset yourself. Come, let me help you to your chamber. I'm sure that you will feel better when you have rested for a while.' Millie escorted their mother from the room. Rose could hear her parent bemoaning the ingratitude of ungrateful daughters until they turned the corner at the end of the passageway.

Her indignation at the unjustified criticism of her beloved faded as she considered the implication of her mother's words. Her parents were still in love; perhaps Papa would listen to his wife and refuse his consent. She could not bear to think of this. To have to wait three long years before she could be with him — she could not bear it. A sick dread settled deep inside. One thing she did know about the man she loved was he would not take kindly to being dismissed by a social inferior. Although she was almost certain he was developing a *tendre* for her, she doubted it would last a three-year separation.

She must put such thoughts aside. Her father was not due back for several weeks and by that time her mother might well have changed her mind again. She would speak to Perry. If he was especially charming he could soon smooth matters over. From now on she too would bite her tongue and behave like the well-mannered daughter her mother wished her to be.

Sir Richard had eyes for no one apart from Millie, thus leaving Rose to entertain her mother as best she could. After several stilted attempts to initiate a conversation Rose abandoned the idea and accepted she was not forgiven. She was forever getting in her mother's bad books. Usually Papa or Millie smoothed things over. Sinking into the far corner of the carriage she mulled over the conversation she'd had with her sister as they were dressing. The ever-romantic Millie had suggested Perry and she elope to Gretna Green. She insisted she and Richard would do so if *they* were forbidden to marry. Rose smiled in the darkness. This was not a solution for her. Imagine! The Duke of

Essex eloping? Never.

Her new ball gown had lived up to her expectations. The confection was even more beautiful than the silver one she had ruined. But somehow, tonight, she did not feel like a princess going to meet her Prince Charming. The disagreement with her mother had cast a pall of gloom over what should have been a joyous occasion.

Flambeaux lit the street and a red carpet led from the pavement to the distant colonnaded portico. Two liveried footmen jumped forward to lower the steps and assist them to alight. Her mama marched ahead, followed by Richard with Millie on his arm. She was left to trail along behind. This was not how she'd expected to have viewed her future home for the first time. She was not one to stand on protocol and disliked the fussy etiquette of society, but this would not do at all.

Just then, down the red carpet strolled her knight in evening clothes. He stood, blocking the path. He nodded politely to her mother who was obliged to pause, thus allowing Rose to catch up.

'Good evening, my love, allow me to escort you.' He gave her mother his most disdainful stare. 'As the future Duchess of Essex it is your prerogative to be at my side to welcome our guests.'

Rose walked past her waiting relatives and slipped her arm through his. He winked at her and then resumed his most aristocratic expression. 'Shall we go? There are friends of mine I wish you to meet. We shall be entertaining them often once we are married.'

He sounded so certain, so confident matters would work out as they wished she almost forgot her fears. She smiled and curtsied and nodded until her face ached. Eventually he drew her to one side. 'You're not yourself tonight, sweetheart. Tell me what's troubling you?'

When she completed her tale, including Millie's suggestion, he laughed. 'Elope? I hardly think that suitable for us. Perhaps for those head over ears in love it might do. We, however, are not so unpleasantly afflicted. We have affection and respect to bond us, do we not, my dear?'

Her dreams were shattered by his casual comment. He did not love her. She had mistaken the matter, read too much into his frequent use of endearments. She hid her misery and asked brightly. 'I would dearly like to see Mop; do we have time before dinner is served?'

'I was about to suggest the same thing. You see, my dear, we shall deal excellently together once we are wed.' He tucked her hand through his crooked arm. 'I have him safe in an empty room. Joseph, a stable boy, is taking care of him.'

The puppy raised his head and thumped his tail when she stepped into the room as if he recognized her. He looked quite different now he was clean, but this made it more apparent how thin he was. 'Do you think he will recover?'

The tousle haired boy replied cheerily. 'Don't you fret, miss, he'll do fine. I reckon in a few days he'll be running about chasing his tail. Tough little beggars, puppies are.'

'I do hope so. I shall come and see him again soon.'

'There, as you can see the patient is making excellent progress. We must not tarry here or we shall be missed.' He paused in the shadows of the vast marble-floored entrance hall.

'I'm glad you have my ring on your finger, my love. I wish everyone here to know you are my future duchess. I also want to say you look *ravisante*. Yet again, I shall be the envy of every gentleman present.' His finger brushed away her tears and he smiled his toe-curling smile. 'Don't cry, sweetheart, Mop will not die. He would not dare, not when he's living in *my* house.'

They led the assembled guests from the grand salon, through the open double doors, into the dining room. Her eyes widened as she took in the splendour of white napery, silver cutlery and glittering crystal ware. The table was big enough to dance on.

He squeezed her arm apologetically. 'I'm sorry, Rose, but tonight you must sit at the far end of this ridiculous table. It's what's expected of us. I can assure you when you are my wife you may arrange things differently, but my sister holds sway at the moment.'

He guided her to her place and strolled off to the far end of the room leaving her to sit in splendid isolation, surrounded by people she didn't know. There were at least fifty at the table. Her mother, Millie and Richard were lost somewhere in the middle of the throng so she couldn't even talk to them.

She had little appetite but tried everything placed in front of her including raw oysters. She thought swallowing these sea creatures virtually alive an unpleasant experience, and one she did not intend to repeat anytime soon. The meal was interminable and by the end she was feeling decidedly queasy. When the final dishes were removed Lady Laura Foster nodded in her direction; time to lead the ladies from the room and leave the gentlemen to their port.

As they emerged into the drawing-room the butler glided up to Mama and passed on a message of some sort. Immediately her mother's expression changed. Her face was radiant and she looked almost like a young woman again. There could be only one explanation — Papa had returned.

'Rosamond, find your sister immediately. We must return home; your father is waiting for us there.'

Millie was equally overjoyed. As they waited for their cloaks her sister whispered in her ear, 'I'm so glad he's home early — he was not expected for several weeks. Are you not happy, Rose?'

'I am, but I can't help thinking about what Mama said earlier today. I fear she will talk Papa into refusing Perry.'

'When you tell Papa how much you love him . . . '

'But I don't, not really — it's more an arrangement between friends. I find myself mistaken in my feelings.'

Her sister looked sceptical but was unable to comment further as their cloaks arrived and they had to follow Mama to the carriage. Her mother was full of animated chatter about how long it had been since she had seen Papa. Even Millie was not able to ask the all-important question — would Papa give his consent to their engagements?

Although not a long journey Rose was feeling extremely unwell by the time they reached home. She had thought the oyster had tasted rather strange. Standing in the open doorway was her father. He jumped down the marble steps and opened the carriage door. He lifted Mama and swung her around just as if she were not decidedly plump. Both Rose and her sister knew better than to interrupt this homecoming. He was loved by all his family, but especially by Mama. Rose would have to wait her turn to greet him, as was only proper. Keeping one arm firmly around Mama's waist he beckoned.

'My darling girls, I had not expected to find you here as well as your mama. You do not normally come to town during the Season. I can see you have grown into beautiful young women in my absence. Quickly, give me a kiss, then join your mother and me in the drawing-room for tea in half an hour.'

He smelt of the sea. His face was tanned nut brown and he was a little slimmer than when she had seen him last.

'Papa, I cannot tell you how pleased I am to see you back safely. Is David with you?'

'No, Rose, but he's not far behind. I left him to deal with customs and other business matters; I could not delay another moment.'

She was feeling more nauseous by the minute. 'Millie, I am going to cast up my accounts. I think the oyster I ate was tainted. It might best if you sleep next door tonight. Please apologize to Papa; I shall speak to him tomorrow when I am well.'

'It's a good thing we came home early. Imagine how horrible it would have been if you had been unwell at the ball.'

Rose could not remain another moment. With her hands clutched over her mouth she fled upstairs not a moment too soon. She spent a miserable few hours before the sickness passed and she was able to sleep. She didn't wake until noon the next day and by then she was too late . . .

★   ★   ★

Perry received the news Rose had gone, and her reason, with mixed emotions. Relief he could now set matters in motion for their marriage and resignation that he must endure the tedium of a ball without his delightful companion at his side. He led Charlotte out for the first set and, duty done, retired to the card room. Sir John Wiggins, the owner of the elusive chestnuts greeted him effusively.

'Bentley, just the man. If you want my nags — then they are yours at the price we agreed earlier.'

Perry shook hands with the gentleman and was well pleased with the deal. He was to take a bank draft round to Wiggins' dwelling tomorrow morning or the horses would go to another eager buyer. On looking up he saw Richard waving to him from the doorway.

'At what time tomorrow morning will you be in Grosvenor Square to make your formal request?'

'I have business to attend to in the morning. I shall go during the afternoon some time. Do you expect him to give his permission?'

'I don't see why not. And in your case, Perry, he would be mad to refuse. You are every parent's dream ... a Duke, and not one in his dotage either.'

'I wish ... ' He had been about to

reveal his true feelings — but that would not do. 'I wish the girls were older. I fear he might refuse on the grounds they are too young for matrimony.'

'Then we have a longer engagement period. I am quite happy to wait.'

No more was said on the matter and Perry made himself scarce until he was needed to bid the guests farewell.

★　★　★

When he got back from delivering the payment for the chestnuts at noon the next day he was well satisfied with his morning's work. He had left himself ample time to change his clothes and prepare his speech before setting out for Grosvenor Square. He bounded up his front steps. As always, an alert footman opened the door before he reached it. His butler was hovering in the entrance hall.

'Your Grace, some items arrived this morning and a letter. I have put them in your study.'

Perry felt a knot settle in his stomach. He opened the door and his worst fears were realized. Stacked tidily on his desk were the jewellery cases. He already knew what he would read in the letter that accompanied these things. Snatching it up he scanned the contents.

Your Grace,
I am returning your gifts with my heartfelt gratitude for your kindness to my daughter in my absence.

I understand her wild behaviour prompted you to act as you did in order to save her reputation. You will, no doubt, be as relieved as she that the reason for you to marry is no longer necessary. I have returned from India a nabob, which means she is a wealthy heiress and will be able to appear in public without fear of being ostracised.

My lawyers will reimburse you immediately for your expenditure on my family's behalf.

*We are removing to the country
for the remainder of the year. However, when I'm next in Town, I hope
I may shake your hand and thank you
in person.*

*Rose is far too young to contem-
plate matrimony for she will not be
one and twenty for a further three
years. When she does return for a full
season you would be very welcome to
call.*

I remain yours sincerely,

With a roar of rage Perry swept the
jewellery from the desk. He had been
dismissed as if of no account. He
was of no further use to her, he was
redundant. He tore the letter to shreds
and scattered it over the spilt contents
of the boxes. He thanked God he had
been saved from making a complete
fool of himself. He would never put
himself in such a position again. In
the short time he had known this girl
she had wheedled her way into his
heart. When he did marry in order to

procreate he would do the choosing and he would make certain he selected a girl he could not fall in love with.

★   ★   ★

'Are you feeling more the thing, my dear? Your papa and I have been most concerned.'

Rose rubbed her eyes and yawned. 'Mama, have you been there long? I am so sorry not to have been able to speak to Papa. I think it might have been the oyster.'

'Very likely; I did not touch them myself. Now, your bath is waiting and so is your papa. Do you feel well enough to join us downstairs?'

'I do, as long as I'm not required to eat anything. I shall be down directly.'

She was surprised to find only her father in the drawing-room. She ran to him and he embraced her fondly.

'Papa, I have so much to tell you.'

'Let me speak first, my dear. When Millie told me why you became

267

engaged to Bentley I own it deeply shocked me. To have behaved in such a way was foolish indeed; another gentleman might not have acted so gallantly.'

He gestured towards the seat and she sat down meekly. She was obviously going to be taken severely to task. Her papa continued: 'However, I am delighted to tell you that your circumstances have changed and you no longer have to make such a sacrifice on my behalf. I have returned a very wealthy man.'

'Papa, I must . . . '

'No, my dear girl, you do not have to thank me. I have returned Lord Bentley's family jewels with my thanks. If he had appeared first thing, as young Devonshire did, we could have discussed matters in person. He is obviously as relieved as you must be your association is at an end.'

Papa believed he had been doing her a favour; she could not tell him he had broken her heart. Blinking back her tears she pinned on a smile. 'I am sure you are correct. Will you excuse me, I am not feeling very well. I must return to my chamber.'

'Of course. We are leaving for the country first thing tomorrow. You should spend today in bed. Millie has already instructed your abigail to begin packing your trunks.'

Feeling like an old woman she stumbled to her feet. There was something she had to know before she left. 'And Millie? What of her betrothal?'

'A different matter entirely, my love. Theirs is a love match, not an arrangement of convenience unsatisfactory to both sides. Devonshire is to remain in Town; they are not allowed to communicate in any way. However, if they are both still of the same mind he will join us in July.'

She nodded. 'I am happy for her. Returning to Hertfordshire is exactly what I want; I do not enjoy the smoke and the smell of the city.'

How glad Rose was that she did not meet her sister or mother on her return to her bed chamber for they would have known at once she was desperately unhappy. She must rally herself, put on a brave face and convince her family she was pleased her engagement had been terminated.

Perry had told her initially he had no feelings for her, but she had begun to believe he loved her as much she loved him. But wouldn't he have been as eager as Devonshire to speak to Papa if he *had* changed his mind? The fact he hadn't come this morning was evidence enough her father had been right. She must console herself with the fact at least he was now free to find someone he could love and not be obliged to marry a girl he had no feelings for.

The following day Rose said little on the journey, but her parents and sister had so much to say they scarcely noticed. Her spirits lifted when the familiar landscape appeared on either side of the carriage. Things would be easier to bear when she was at home.

'Rose, are you still feeling nauseous?'

'I am, Mama, the motion of the

carriage has disturbed my stomach. I shall be glad to arrive and have firm ground under my feet once more.'

This explanation appeared to satisfy them all, and her parents made no objection when she retired to her bed chamber. In the country she and Millie had adjoining apartments; only in London did they share. Mary was waiting for her. As usual the trunks and staff had left the previous evening, as had the groom with her mare.

'My, you look very pale, miss, I think you would be best in bed.'

Rose didn't argue. With the curtains drawn around her she could cry without fear of being overheard. She didn't understand how in such a short space of time her feelings could have changed from infatuation, to dislike, and then to real love. There would never be another. If she could not marry Perry she would remain a spinster.

15

The weeks dragged by. However much she tried to raise her flagging spirits Rose remained unnaturally quiet. Even her daily rides did nothing to restore her happiness. Mama was unusually solicitous and watched her anxiously. As the date for her shared anniversary approached she was summoned to her mother's sitting-room. Millie had gone to visit friends in the village.

'My dear, come and sit down. Your father and I have come up with a scheme to celebrate your birthdays. We do hope this is something you will be happy with.'

'I'm sure whatever you suggest will be ideal.'

'We thought to invite all our tenants and the village folk, as well as our friends and neighbours, to an outdoor celebration of some sort. What do you think?'

Rose made an effort to appear excited. 'A garden party, Mama? That would be lovely — it's been too long since we opened the grounds to the village.'

'I shall need your help to organise it for I fear we have left it rather late. Only two weeks until your name days. This is hardly long enough to arrange everything satisfactorily.'

For the first time in many weeks Rose felt a surge of enthusiasm. There was nothing she liked better than a challenge. 'Millie has always loved the stilt walkers and fire eaters who appear at the village fair occasionally. We must have those. I should like a Punch and Judy for the children and could we not have a horse race around the park for the gentlemen?'

'We shall have whatever you want; no expense is to be spared. I believe I can leave the entertainment in your capable hands. I shall concentrate on providing sufficient food and drink for the several hundred people who might attend.'

'Millie must be involved. She can design some posters so our guests know what treats are in store for them.' She jumped up and rushed over to hug her mother.

'Thank you, and please thank Papa. I know why you have suggested this, and you're quite right to think I need an interest to pull me out of my low spirits.'

This was the first time she had admitted out loud she had not been herself. She waited for the inevitable question.

'Has something been troubling you, my dear? You have been very subdued since we returned from London. Millie suggested this was because you believe your reputation will be in ruins and you will not be able to attend another Season.'

This was as good an explanation as any. Something was certainly destroyed. She would never reveal to her parents that her father's well-meaning interference was the cause of her unhappiness.

'I am delighted to be able to tell you, my dear girl, that nothing could be further from the case. The letter we had from your brother last week said everyone is sympathetic to your plight. Your papa is the villain of the piece. He has been blamed for refusing his permission. Lord Bentley has left town also and they are saying he is suffering from a broken heart.'

'I can assure you he is more likely to be suffering from hurt pride. He has a very high opinion of himself, you know.'

Her mother stared at her as if she were a simpleton. 'I should think he does, my dear. Would not anyone born into his position feel the same? Good heavens, if a Duke cannot be proud of his heritage, then who can?'

'All this is irrelevant anyway; my opinion is neither here nor there. Now, I shall get pen and paper and start compiling my list. Remember, Mama, we are going to require several marquees in case the weather is inclement.'

'It would not dare to rain on such an

important day, but marquees we shall have if that is what you want. Have you any preferences for the buffet?'

Rose shuddered. 'As long as there is nothing remotely connected to the sea, I shall be content. Perhaps it would be better to keep it simple. Why not choose food that is unlikely to become tainted if the weather is warm? Fresh bread, cheese and pickles, meat pasties — that sort of thing.' Her mouth began watering at the very thought. 'Some freshly baked scones, apple turnovers, rock cakes and sugared buns would be perfect.

'And to drink — fresh lemonade, porter and small beer. There, all I have to do is arrange for the village baker to help out. Cook could not possibly produce sufficient to feed so many.'

Rose was occupied for the rest of the day with her lists. Papa wandered in to see how she was doing when she failed to appear for afternoon tea.

'How are you progressing, my love? Is there anything you would like your papa to do, apart from pay the trades-men's bills?'

'I wondered if I could have the assistance of Mr. Burton, the estate manager? He's better placed than I to seek out the entertainers I wish to employ. Millie is determined not only to have the fire eaters and stilt walkers but also candied apples, hoopla and a fortune teller. I am at a loss to know where I might find the latter.'

He kissed the top of her head affectionately. 'I know exactly where to find one. There's a Romany encamp-ment on the edge of this estate. I'm certain they will have such a person.' He read over her shoulder. 'A horse race? What an excellent idea, now that's something I shall enjoy watching. What are your entry requirements to be?' He winked at her; he understood her so well.

'As long as I am able to enter on Orion, I care not for the rules. I don't believe there's a horse anywhere that can beat her.' Her smile faded, there was one who could but she was unlikely ever to see Lucifer again. 'And no whips or spurs to be allowed by any participant.'

'Actually, my dear, I came to tell you David's joining us for the remainder of the year. Our business is completed and he no longer needs to reside in Town.'

She hugged her father. 'Wonderful news. David has not spent nearly enough time here since you both returned.' Stepping away she smiled anxiously. 'You will not mind if I race, Papa? I shall be riding astride.'

'My darling daughter, on my land you may do as you please and I dare anyone to criticise. Anyway, that divided skirt you wear reveals little of your person. In fact, far less than some of the gowns I've seen you in. Your divided skirt is perfectly acceptable in my opinion.'

'Are there any cakes left? I find my appetite is restored. I believe I am over my malaise; all it needed was something to look forward to.'

★ ★ ★

Perry felt his fishing rod bend as a fat trout took hold and with an expert flick he tossed the fish on to the riverbank. As he stooped to remove the hook he saw two horsemen cantering towards him across thc field. The setting sun haloed them in golden light. He rubbed his eyes. He had been praying (not something he was used to doing) a lot of late for the intervention of the Almighty. These riders looked like angels sent to his assistance. Good grief! He had spent too long in the sun today; his mind was wandering. Coming towards him were none other than his friends David and Richard. Mop barked a greeting and bounded off to meet his unexpected visitors.

'Good evening to you both. I can't tell you how pleased I am to see you. I have spent too much time alone these past weeks and I am ready for good company. You're just in time for supper.'

Lucifer, who had been grazing in the shadow of the overhanging trees, whickered and trotted up as if he too was pleased to see them.

'Fresh trout, splendid. I'm starving. We didn't stop for lunch today.' David swung from the saddle and tethered his mount to a nearby branch. 'You look like a gypsy, Perry. I can't remember ever seeing you in shirt sleeves and bare feet before.'

David joined him. 'You're thinner, but none the worse for that. What have you been doing with yourself down here in rural isolation?'

Perry deftly gutted the fish he had just caught. 'As you see, I have been fishing; also riding, walking, attending to estate business — and doing more thinking than is good for me.'

David removed his topcoat and sat down to pull off his boots. His stockings followed. 'That's better. Is the water safe to drink?'

'I can do better than that, my friend. If you look to your right you will see a rope, there are a couple of large crocks on the end. One contains beer, the other butter, cheese and freshly cut asparagus.'

He left his friends to reel in these items whilst he busied himself striking the tinderbox and lighting the kindling under the fire he had built earlier. Soon the sticks were burning brightly. He reached into the hedge and removed a large skillet. 'Do you have the butter?'

Richard had run his knife around the wax seal on both the crocks. 'Is there bread to go with this?'

'In the hedge in the basket. If you two would set out the cutlery and crockery, I shall prepare our meal.' The butter melted with a hiss and the appetising aroma of frying trout filled the evening air. Perry had done this so often lately he thought nothing of his culinary skills. Sprinkling salt and chopped herbs across the fish he flipped them over and sat back with a sigh of satisfaction.

'No one would believe the Duke of

Essex sits on his backside on the damp grass whilst he cooks his own supper. You have changed, Perry, and for the better.'

'I have, David, your sister taught me a salutary lesson. Before I met her I believed, I suppose, I was the centre of the universe and I could have anything I desired. Rose is the only thing I've ever wanted that I was denied.'

Richard was rummaging in the basket happily removing its contents. First the two crisp loaves, then a dish of hothouse peaches and finally a pot of chutney appeared.

'Here, David, take these. I have to get out a tablecloth, napkins and the cutlery and crockery.'

'You will find glasses somewhere as well. I'm surprised you haven't seen the two bottles of claret. If you uncork one of those we shall drink a toast to the reunion of old friends.'

By the time they had finished their meal the sun had set. The glorious sound of nightingales filled the air, everywhere was bathed in silver moonlight. For the first time since Rose had sent him away his mood was less bleak. David added more wood to the fire; nobody seemed in any hurry to return. The other horses had been untacked and left to roam some time ago. Perry could see them close by munching happily on the dew-wet grass. He had to ask, he must know how Rose was.

He scratched the puppy's head, keeping his face averted and his voice bland. 'How is your family, David?'

'Millie is well enough. However I hear from my father Rose is not herself.' His friend sat up and looked at him squarely. 'Why have you not gone down to see her instead of moping about here?'

Perry shrugged. 'I was dismissed. Bannerman sent me a letter explaining your sister no longer wished to marry me as the family fortunes were restored. I admit freely that initially the engagement was no more than a convenient arrangement for me, but that changed.

I had thought she felt the same, but obviously I was mistaken. As I said earlier, it did not occur to me anyone would reject the Duke of Essex.'

'You misunderstood. If you had gone to enquire you would have heard what happened. Rose was struck down by food poisoning and did not rise until after the letter had been sent. She knew nothing about matters until after the event.'

'But how did Bannerman know I had offered for her unwillingly?'

'Millie was in Rose's confidence, and she told Papa. Rose has not said she is in love with you; but she *was* miserable for weeks. The last I heard she's recovering.'

'Why the devil didn't she tell him? Surely your parents would not wish her to suffer unnecessarily?'

'The letter I received from Millie said Rose does not want to upset our father. Rose is convinced you would have come to her, as Richard came, if you had truly loved her. You are a nincompoop. You have let the love of your life slip through your fingers. I always knew your pride would be your downfall.'

Perry swung round to face his other friend. 'You knew I had to be elsewhere in the morning, did it not occur to you to tell Bannerman I was intending to come that afternoon?'

Richard recoiled. 'Steady on, you don't know the whole. I was given my marching orders as well. Bannerman said Millie was too young to think of becoming betrothed. I am not to contact her in any way until the summer. From what David tells me, she is not languishing at home, but gadding about enjoying herself. I fear I might have missed my opportunity as well.'

Perry felt ashamed of his anger. 'I'm sorry. You must be in pain too. Now, did you just come to discover how I was, or have you other business here?'

'Actually I came to tell you about a horse race to be held in Hertfordshire in a couple of weeks. There is a horse running that has never been beaten, and a fortune has already been placed on its head. I thought your Lucifer, a genuine dark horse, could run against it and make Richard a wealthy man.'

'I should be eternally grateful Perry, for my inheritance is not great. The odds I would get on Lucifer could ensure I had a few extra thousand to offer when I go to see Lord Bannerman.'

'I should be delighted to assist. It would do no harm to Lucifer's stud fees either. Where exactly does this race take place, David?'

'Around an estate, it moves from place to place each year. I'm not exactly certain on whose land it will be this July. I shall let you know nearer the time. There's an excellent hostelry in St Albans, shall I reserve rooms for you there?'

Perry scooped up a jug of river water and tossed it on the fire. 'Please do. Now, they will be sending out search parties soon if we don't return. We need to gather the debris and put it under the hedge, someone will collect it tomorrow morning.'

He whistled and his stallion loomed out of the darkness. 'I shall leave you to tack up your mounts, Lucifer and I travel light.' Grasping a handful of wiry mane he vaulted on the stallion's back. Then he reached down and grabbed Mop's scruff. The house was too far away for the little dog to run. His mount needed no urging, he was as eager as Perry to return to Bentley Hall. He was not happy; he would never be truly content again. But having something to look forward to, even an event as trivial as a country race, was what he needed to snap out of his melancholy. He must believe somehow he might be given another opportunity to win back the girl he would love for the rest of his life.

16

At last — the big day had arrived. Rose was out of bed in a trice. There was so much to do before the guests started to arrive at noon. Millie had suggested they wear identical outfits for their name day but as they had such dissimilar taste Rose had been uncertain. However, Papa had sent for a seamstress from London and a lovely compromise had been found. She paused to admire her gown in cornflower blue. The sash was in a darker shade and the same colour ribbon encircled her elegant, narrow brimmed bonnet. Dainty, matching blue walking slippers made up the ensemble. Millie's outfit was in primrose, her sash and bonnet ribbon in buttercup yellow. There were also parasols and reticules of the same fabric as the dress, but Rose doubted she would use either of them. Her crisp shirt and divided skirt were far more attractive. Her riding boots were polished to a high shine, the necessary under garments neatly folded beside them. For now she pulled on an old cotton morning dress and pushed her feet into sturdy boots. She would be back to take a bath and change an hour before the birthday party started.

'Happy birthday, my darling girl. Give your old papa a kiss this fine morning.'

'I am so excited. Do you know, David said there are more than thirty entries for the race? I'm glad he's home and has taken over the organisation of this event.'

'Are you coming to eat, Rose?'

'Not yet, Papa. I wish to check the marquees are ready and the stalls are in their correct places. I also have to visit the stable to see Orion has eaten her oats.'

'Then I shall come with you. I must say it's decidedly strange not having a house full of guests. But as you and

Millie were so insistent we only invite those who could travel the house is empty. Your mama and I wish you to have exactly what you want on your special day.'

A clatter on the stairs heralded the arrival of her sister. 'Wait for me, I want to see everything as well.' Whilst Papa embraced Millie, Rose waited on the front step.

'Look at that. The park looks like a scene from a storybook, not like our grounds at all. And we have perfect weather and there are even a few bluebells still flowering just for us.'

Millie came out to join her on the steps. 'Have you any idea what we are to receive as our gift?'

'None at all; all Papa would say is that our gifts would arrive this afternoon. I have more than enough already. I think of this party as my present.'

There was one thing she would like above anything to make her day perfect, but arranging that was not within her father's remit. After the first three weeks her sister had no longer mentioned Richard, and now had several young gentlemen in tow.

'Which of your admirers is to escort you today, Millie?' Rose asked quietly.

'I have invited none of them. I am in love with Richard. I'm counting the days until he's allowed to come here.'

'Well, girls, where are we to look first?'

★ ★ ★

Outside, the sound of hammering, shouting and raucous laughter indicated the stall holders were busy at their tasks. Rose stepped out of her bath and into the towel held out for her by Mary. Daisy had been appointed to take care of her sister. Mama had insisted they were old enough to require their own abigails.

'Not a cloud in the sky, miss, the good Lord has blessed this day, that's for sure.'

'I want everyone to enjoy themselves.

I love to see people happy, it raises my own spirits wonderfully.'

Her maid snorted. 'Begging your pardon, miss, I think it's shameful you were let down so badly . . . '

'Mary, I've asked you before not to talk about that matter. It's in the past; today I believe I can move on with my life.'

Stepping into the high-waisted gown made her feel elegant, beautiful even. She'd not had that feeling since she wore the silver confection *he* had given her. She never said his name, even in her head it made her eyes fill with unwanted tears. She was well aware it might take years, not weeks, to recover from her disappointment.

Millie burst into the bedroom. 'Hurry up, Rose, you are tardy.'

'I'm ready now. Although we are quite different in many ways, today we actually look like twins.'

Arm in arm they ran downstairs to where their parents were waiting for them.

'Darling girls, you have both changed out of all recognition these past few months. I have two grown-up daughters now to go with my adult son.'

'Where is David? I thought it strange of him to stay away with his friends the night before our party.'

'As you did not wish anyone to stay here, and he has invited a few cronies down for the race, he had no choice but to stay elsewhere.' Her mama smiled fondly. 'I'm sure he will be here in good time. After all they are only staying in the next village.'

Already the grounds were filling up with local people, the children squealing with excitement and running from booth to booth. Today the sugar treats, ribbons and fancies were not for sale — they were to be given free. Every child would be given three tickets to exchange for whatever they wished.

She could not be sad with so many smiling faces everywhere. The next hour sped by. The race was to be run at one o'clock. An air of eager anticipation rippled around the spectators. David had told Rose thousands of guineas had been bet on the outcome; she wished Orion was not the favourite. She did not approve of gambling as this led inevitably to disappointment and disaster. If she'd had her way there'd have been no bets placed.

'I must get ready for I can see the other riders are already milling about at the starting line. I'm so glad I did not have anything to eat.'

The house was cool and dark, the noise from outside muted. She ran lightly up the massive staircase and into her bed chamber. Mary had been given the afternoon off. Rose was quite capable of dressing herself when she had to.

Placing her gown on the bed she stripped off her petticoats and stepped into her navy blue, divided skirt. A white cotton shirt followed and a handsome cornflower blue waistcoat topped the outfit. The number she had been allotted was painted on a square of card and this she tied around her waist. Her boots nowadays were loose, but this made it easier to pull them on.

She uncoiled her plait from her head and tied a bright blue ribbon around the end. Picking up her gloves she dashed down the servants' staircase and out through the side door which led to the stables.

Orion whinnied and stamped her hooves. 'Wait one more moment, sweetheart, I must check your girth is firm.'

The stable yard was empty of humans; all the staff had permission to attend the party. Leading her mare from the loose box to the mounting block Rose felt a moment's doubt. What if she took a tumble in front of those who had risked their hard-earned cash in the belief that she could win? Thirty entries! David had told her some had even come from London. July was a slack time in the social calendar and wealthy gentlemen were always looking for entertainment.

Her horse butted her gently as if to remind her the time had come to depart. Blue ribbons had been plaited into the animal's mane; her dapple grey coat gleamed with health. In one fluid movement Rose settled into the saddle, pushed her boots into the stirrups, clicked her tongue and they were trotting to join the others. In the melee at the starting line she couldn't see to see who was who. Several riders greeted her by name, others touched their hats. She felt decidedly underdressed compared to the splendour of some of the entrants. Too late to repine. David was calling them to order.

The entry numbers had been picked out of a hat and each rider allocated a position. She was in the second row, an ideal place, Orion ran better when coming from behind. She was hard pressed to keep the mare still as she was dancing on the spot, straining against the bit, desperate to be off like all the other horses.

The ribbon was up and they were

away. Racing against one or two horses had not prepared her for this. She couldn't see in front of her. The dust and dirt flying up all but choked her. Her heart pounded. She didn't know which way to direct Orion — at any moment she could be buffeted from the saddle. Nobody cared she was the only female entrant — in a race like this every rider must take care of himself. Then she saw a glimmer of grass to her right — a small space through which her agile mare could thunder.

'Go on, Orion, this is our chance.'

Crouching in the saddle she threw her hands forward and her mount took off like a grey arrow. In front of her was open track — she was in the lead. The only way she could win this race was if she stayed in front. The larger horses would hedge her in if she allowed them to. Her plait streamed out behind her, wind whipped tears from her eyes. She was flying. One more bend and she would be in the home straight. The noise from the other horses was fading.

Only the sound of the spectators on either side accompanied her wild ride. Orion must be twenty yards or more ahead of her nearest rival. Nothing could beat her now. The screaming crowd was urging Rose on — she could see the finish post less than one hundred yards away.

Then the mare's ears flattened, she stuck out her nose and renewed her effort. A black nose edged past Rose's boot. She couldn't believe it. She glanced sideways to see a man she almost didn't recognize riding Lucifer. Perry was in shirt sleeves, his hair blowing wildly. He was laughing with exhilaration and obviously thought he could beat her. Standing in her stirrups, Rose threw her weight forward, screaming at her horse to make one last effort. Lucifer was inching closer, he was going to win . . .

The finish post flashed past. She had no idea which of them had crossed it first. It took a further fifty yards to slow the horses to a walk. On either side of the track men were throwing their hats in the air, hugging each other and dancing wildly. Did this mean she was the victor? Two well-remembered arms reached up and lifted her from the saddle.

'The race was a dead heat. We passed the line together. I can't believe it. Lucifer has never been equalled before.'

★ ★ ★

Rose's shirt was sticking to her, she was mud-streaked and dishevelled and he had never seen anything so beautiful.

'My darling, I love you to distraction. I have been wretched without you. Can you forgive me for my neglect and let me back into your life?'

'I have been miserable also. I did not know that anything could hurt as much as losing you. I love you, Perry. I have done so for the past five years and will do so until the day I die.'

Without a second thought he dropped

to one knee in front of her. 'Rose, will you marry me? I cannot live without you.'

Her face was radiant, her remarkable eyes huge. 'I will, of course I will.'

Oblivious to the gawping spectators he crushed her to his heart. She tilted her face and stretched up to receive his kiss.

★ ★ ★

She wanted the embrace to last forever. She pressed closer wishing to show him how much she had missed him; how happy she was to see him. They were squashed between the bulk of their sweating mounts and the pressure was making it increasingly difficult to breathe.

'I think this must wait until later. We must go and receive the winner's reward. The race is not over until we have done that.'

'We shall share the glory and the prize money. Don't you think, my love, that it is the perfect start to our betrothal?'

He tossed her into the saddle. 'I do, darling girl, and there's something else that you don't know. Shall I tell you a secret?' He spoke from beside her, re-mounted on his stallion. 'It would appear I am your name day gift. Richard is also here, for Millie.'

'So we have my father's blessing this time?' They were trotting towards the wooden platform which had been constructed to hand out the prizes. 'How long have you known?'

'Not until I arrived here last night. David invited me to race, but failed to mention where the event was taking place. Your father was waiting at the inn.' He stretched across and touched her cheek. His smile made her head swim.

'You're the image of him, as your sister is of your mother. Although he's reluctant to let you go, he wishes you to be happy and realizes you will never be so kept apart from me.'

A cheer greeted their arrival to collect the ribbons and the cup. Unexpectedly shy, Rose hung back. 'You collect the prize for us. I shall remain here and wait. High time I practised being a subservient wife.'

'When you are that I shall sprout wings and fly.'

With his hair curling wildly on his collar he looked like a buccaneer from a storybook. Her heart was bursting with happiness — she loved him so much. She smiled at his appearance. His apparel was dishevelled and he had as much mud on his person as she had on hers. He was no longer an austere and unapproachable aristocrat; he was instead the man of her dreams.

After the presentation the crowd returned to the jollifications and they were able to retire to the stables to steal a few precious moments together before joining her family in the house. She slid to the ground and turned to lead her exhausted mare into the waiting loose box knowing Perry was close behind. A shaggy dog all but knocked her off her feet.

'Mop! You've brought him with you. He looks so well, he's the best present I've ever had.'

'I'm mortally offended, my darling. I thought nothing could match me when it came to name day gifts.'

Still laughing at the dog's antics she held out her hand and he pulled her to her feet. She swayed towards him. Pounding feet interrupted them as two grinning stable boys arrived. The larger of the two spoke up. 'The master says we is to take care of the horses, miss, he's a-waiting for you up at the house.'

Perry's arm enfolded her waist. 'Come my darling, we have the rest of our lives to be together. Your family wants to celebrate our happiness with us.'

She tilted her face to stare at him. 'I can hardly believe you are really here with me. I thought never to see you again.'

Ignoring the curious eyes of the lads he swept her from her feet. 'My darling,

I give you my word that I shall never leave you alone again. If you would like me to I shall obtain a special licence and we can be married immediately. What do you think?'

In answer she pulled his dear head down and kissed him. When eventually she drew breath his shout of triumph sent the stable cat hissing and spitting up a tree. He spun her round in his arms until she was dizzy.

'Enough, Perry my love, the stable boys think you have run mad.'

His mouth covered hers again in a hard kiss. 'I care not what anyone says. From now on we shall do as we like and if society doesn't like it then so be it. Your love has liberated me; in future I intend to be as unconventional as you.'

'And I, my love, have decided to be sensible, as befits my new status.'

He dropped her gently to the ground and, hand in hand, they ran towards the house like children recently released from school. The Duke of Essex was no longer proud and disdainful and Rose Bannerman was no longer prejudiced and wild. True love, as it always does, has changed them both.

THE END

We do hope that you have enjoyed reading this large print book.

Did you know that all of our titles are available for purchase?

We publish a wide range of high quality large print books including:
Romances, Mysteries, Classics
General Fiction
Non Fiction and Westerns

Special interest titles available in large print are:
The Little Oxford Dictionary
Music Book, Song Book
Hymn Book, Service Book

Also available from us courtesy of Oxford University Press:
Young Readers' Dictionary
(large print edition)
Young Readers' Thesaurus
(large print edition)

For further information or a free brochure, please contact us at:
Ulverscroft Large Print Books Ltd.,
The Green, Bradgate Road, Anstey,
Leicester, LE7 7FU, England.
Tel: (00 44) **0116 236 4325**
Fax: (00 44) **0116 234 0205**